TRASHY

(a *Take It Off* novel)

She's trying to move on, but the past won't let her go.

I fell in love once.

It was a big mistake, but the biggest mistake of all was staying with him.

He pushed me around. He cheated and treated me like trash.

I don't feel sorry for myself, because I let him.

But no more.

I moved out. I'm saving my stripper's salary for an education that will get me somewhere better.

But breaking the chains of a shitty past isn't easy. He says I owe him. He says we aren't done. I don't care what he says anymore.

I do care about Adam.

But my history tells me I'm not the best judge of men. And the fact Adam's been married four times tells me he probably isn't a safe choice.

I need safe. I need better. I need out.

If the past is any indication of my future, getting out isn't going to be easy.

TRASHY

Take It Off Series

CAMBRIA HEBERT

http://www.cambriahebert.com

Interior design and typesetting by Sharon Kay
Cover design by MAE I DESIGN
Edited by Cassie McCown
Copyright 2014 by Cambria Hebert

ISBN: 978-1-938857-58-4

Other books by Cambria Hebert

Heven & Hell Series

Before
Masquerade
Between
Charade
Bewitched
Tirade
Beneath
Renegade
Heven & Hell Anthology

Take It Off Series

Torch
Tease
Tempt
Text
Tipsy
Tricks
Tattoo
Tryst
Taste

Standalone Titles

Distant Desires
Blank
Whiteout

Death Escort Series

Recalled
Charmed

DEDICATION

I always said I wanted to write a "trashy" novel.

Guess I can check that off the bucket list. ☺

TRASHY

PROLOGUE

Roxie

High school…

The distinct sound of bowling balls cracking against pins reverberated through the entire building, echoing out the door and into the parking lot. We stood by a row of cars while a couple people in our group smoked the last of their cigarettes before going in to claim our lane.

I lived in a small town; most people probably didn't even know it was on the map. It was surrounded by mountains and had just as many bars as it did churches. The economy here sucked, and it seemed like the general population was aging. The young people could be broken down into two groups:

1) Those who got stuck here and never left
and
2) Those who got out and never came back

The unfortunate people who fell into group one usually worked in jobs they hated for too little pay and grew more bitter as they aged.

I planned on being in group two and getting the hell out of here as soon as I could. Like right after high school. There had to be more out there than this.

I'd worked hard to keep up my grades. I'd kept my nose clean and stayed away from drugs. Two more years and I could bid this town good-bye and start over, hopefully somewhere warmer.

"Can we go in?" I said. "It's freezing out here."

January in a tiny town in Maryland was one reason I would never smoke. Who wanted to stand outside in the freezing cold just to get a fix?

"Hey, we're going in!" Lena yelled out, and we started up the little ramp that led inside. Lena and I had been best friends since middle school when we were randomly sat at the same table. She was outgoing and didn't seem to mind I wasn't. We became fast friends, and she introduced me to her circle, who, in turn, became my friends too.

Lena was the pretty one. The one who always got sidelong glances from the guys in the hallway. When a school dance was held, she always had offers, always had a date.

I was sort of invisible beside her.

Okay, people saw me. It wasn't as if I were a ghost. But I wasn't really the main attraction. No guy ever looked at me just a little too long because I'd caught his eye. Every guy I'd ever crushed on thought of me like a sister or didn't even know I existed. I'd never been to a school dance because no one ever asked me.

Yeah, I could go alone.

How pathetic would that be?

I pretended I didn't want to go. I pretended school dances just weren't my thing. But they were my thing. And every time the sweetheart dance or homecoming dance would roll around, something inside me would shrink just a little, because no one thought I would make a good date.

I liked to think that I was waiting, that no other guy would matter until the right one came along. That the guy who noticed me first, the one who stared just a little too long… he was the one who mattered. He was the one who deserved my heart.

Besides, falling in love in this town would just make my plan of getting the hell out even harder. I wanted love. I wanted to see that look in someone's eye; you know, the look where you are their entire world.

But I wanted out of here more.

Inside, the center was packed. If we hadn't reserved a lane for cyber bowling, we wouldn't have gotten one. Cyber bowling was one of the town's only things to do here on the weekend, besides getting drunk and partying at someone's house whose parents weren't home.

And we did plenty of that.

But sometimes we wanted to get out. To see and be seen.

Bowling at midnight on a Friday, with nothing but black lights, flashing strobes, and a blaring jukebox, was the way to do it.

Yes. I found it extremely ironic that we went out to see and be seen where they shut off all the lights.

There used to be a club, a teen club, just fifteen minutes up the road. It was the kind of place we couldn't go to without our male friends, because a group of girls there alone was ripe for the picking. Your ass got grabbed; you got propositioned; you got leered at. One time I got hauled onto the dance floor by some drunk guy (who likely was not a teenager) who locked his arms around me and refused to let go.

I'm pretty sure he wasn't the guy I'd been waiting for all my life.

Gross.

"You know you want these," Lena said, handing over a pair of ass-ugly brown loafers that Velcro-ed closed.

"Girl, I am going to rock these," I quipped and strutted over to our lane.

She laughed and followed along. A couple guys a few lanes away whistled at her.

Lena had long, thick blond hair, curves that probably made her daddy crazy, and a laugh that made you think she had quite a bit of naughty under all that nice.

I had plain brown hair, plain brown eyes, and the only curves I had were from the cell phone in the back pocket of my jeans.

"Did we get two lanes?" I asked, glancing at the one right beside ours. It was empty too.

"Christy invited her boyfriend. He's bringing his friends," Lena said, strapping on her ugly shoes.

Christy was another friend of ours. She was dating a senior at the other high school here in this town. I'd seen him around, but never really talked to him. My stomach felt a little funny thinking about a whole lane of guys we didn't know next to us all night. Not that it mattered. They would all fall over Lena when they saw her.

The rest of our friends filtered in from the cold, and we all stood around laughing and poking fun at each other and our ugly feet. Christy was sitting on her boyfriend's lap when several guys walked up. Kevin (Christy's boyfriend) stood and gave them all high-fives and fist-bumps.

I swear cavemen probably did the same thing back in the day when they clubbed their dinner and dragged it home.

I turned away and started entering names into the screens overhead, the one that kept our scores. Bowling started in like five minutes and someone had to do this. After I filled out our lane's lineup, I switched over to Kevin's, typing in his name first.

Lena came up beside me, a guy right behind her. "This is Ben," she said.

I gave him a wave and typed in his name.

"There is also a PJ, Chris, and…" Lena's voice trailed off as she looked toward the group of guys, trying to see who else was here.

"I don't know the other guy's name," she whispered.

Ben had already wandered off to find a ball.

"He can type it in," I said, stepping away from the computer.

"It's Craig," a low voice whispered in my ear.

His breath feathered over my ear, causing my eyes to droop just a little. Goosebumps raced down my spine and filled my toes, making them tingle.

I turned to glance over my shoulder.

He had blue eyes.

He was still incredibly close.

"What?" I said, unable to look away.

"My name," he said, giving me a half smile. "For the screen." He motioned, reminding me it was there.

"Oh," I said. "Right."

He grinned. He had a dimple on each side of his mouth. Broad shoulders. Full lips. And a backward baseball hat pulled over his forehead.

I was staring.

I couldn't *not* stare at him.

"You any good at bowling?" he asked.

How had I not seen him around before? Where the hell had he been?

"The best," I said. "I always win."

He flashed a grin. "Not tonight. I don't lose. Especially to a girl."

Is he flirting with me?

"Roxie," Lena called, stepping up to my side. "You're up."

This was the part where I would lose his attention. This was the part where he saw he had better options.

He gave Lena the *what up* gesture with his chin.

He kept his eyes on me.

He kept his eyes on me.

I smiled. "I hope your ego can handle it when you lose tonight. Especially to a girl," I told him.

"Game on," he said, backing toward his lane, not once looking away.

Butterflies lifted their wings and took flight in my belly.

Lena pulled me away and shoved me near the thingy that returned your ball. Cool air blew up from the vent, causing a few strands of my hair to float out around me.

"You know him?" she whispered.

"No. Do you?" I whispered back.

"Just that he's a friend of Kevin's."

I nodded. I didn't tell her how hot I thought he was. I didn't mention the freaking butterfly sanctuary inside my middle. I calmly picked up the ball I was going to use and walked toward the center dot in front of the lane.

I would be silly to mention it when I knew he probably wasn't interested.

Before I overthought it, I stole a glance over my shoulder. He was sitting in the chairs, laughing at something one of the guys said. His dimples were on full display.

But even though he was having a conversation with them, he was still looking at me.

I looked away. A little thrill of something shot through me. I stared down at the pins, barely even registering them.

Maybe he's the one you've been waiting for, my heart whispered.

I couldn't have been more wrong.

1

Roxie

Present Day

A creepy feeling crawled over my skin, making me shiver and smack at my arms like there was some long-legged hairy spider climbing its way over my body. I abandoned what I was doing and stood, cocking my head to the side to listen. There was nothing out of the ordinary. The only sound that filled the air was the insistent hum of the clothes dryer.

There were no heavy footfalls echoing down the steps. No ominous sounds of heavy breathing reached my ears (Come on, you know creepy, no-good people all breathe heavily).

My phone went off, making me jump and let out a little shriek.

I was being ridiculous. I was being paranoid.

One glance at the screen and the number I didn't recognize and my belly did a little nosedive. After disregarding the gut feeling of being watched, I hit the IGNORE button and dropped the cell into the bottom of the basket. Not caring if my clothes were completely dry, I wrenched open the dryer and pulled out the pile of damp fabric, dumping it into a heap on top of the stuff I'd already folded. I'd had enough of laundry to last me a lifetime. 'Course, maybe I wouldn't hate the chore so much if I didn't have to haul it all across the parking lot and down two flights of stairs.

What was it with landlords? Did they all get together one night and decide they would put their laundry facilities in the grossest, most inconvenient places possible just to torture the tenants?

There are worse things in life than having to hike a mile to wash your clothes. I snorted at the thought because it was so true.

It was hot down here in this laundry basement. The running dryers and crappy ventilation made the air feel stuffy and hot. It didn't help that it was humid as hell outside, with a thunderstorm threatening overhead, promising a torrential downpour at any given moment.

After adding my little plastic jug of detergent and dryer sheets into the basket with the clean clothes, I piled it on top of another full, identical basket and hefted them into my arms. After trudging up two flights of steps, I pushed through the door and stepped outside, the humid air not offering the slightest relief from being in that basement.

With a sigh, I headed toward the apartment I shared with my roommate, Harlow. A flash of neon lightning lit up the deep purple-hued sky, reminding me of a strobe light the DJ sometimes turned on at the club.

A sudden colossal boom of thunder caused my body to jerk, and one of my socks fell from the basket and landed on the sidewalk.

"Ugh," I spat and set the baskets on the ground to fetch my runaway sock. The sound of squealing tires cut through the parking lot, and I jumped up, spinning around with a pounding heart and searching the darkened lot with wide eyes.

It wasn't late enough to be dark, but this storm was doing a damn good job of hiding the sun and all the light it provided.

On the other side of the parking lot, a red car sped around the corner and disappeared. I blew out a breath and shook my head at my own paranoid behavior. I really needed to quit being so jumpy.

You have a reason to be jumpy, a voice in my head whispered.

After grabbing up the baskets once more, I walked the rest of the way to my apartment and up the stairs. Once inside, I dumped the baskets on the floor and went in the kitchen for a cold water and eyed the contents of the fridge as I drained half the bottle.

We were running low on food.

I smiled. Cam called it girl food. Cam and Harlow had been together for months now, and he split his time between here and his place. Since he stayed so often we kept Pop-tarts and bacon around because that was his version of man food.

It was my turn to do the shopping since Harlow went last week. I'd just add that to the list of chores I did not want to do. The digital clock on the microwave stared at me, the red numbers jumping out as if to remind me I was going to be late if I didn't hurry up.

After setting my cell on the kitchen counter, I took my laundry into my room and set it beside the bed. It was clean. It was folded (well, most of it). I could put it away later. I moved quickly, almost on autopilot, and unzipped my duffle bag to toss in a couple handfuls of clothing. I didn't even pay attention to what outfits I was packing. It really didn't matter. They were all basically the same anyway.

When a girl worked as a stripper, the only important part about her wardrobe was that it came off easily.

Once that was finished, I grabbed a simple cotton dress, a pair of panties, and went into the bathroom to take a shower. I felt gross after doing laundry and chores all day. Hopefully a cold shower would freshen me up a bit and get me ready for tonight.

I wasn't new to being a stripper. I'd been taking off my clothes for money for a couple years now. Even still, sometimes the fact that this was my life still shocked the hell out of me.

How did I get here?

It was a question I asked myself a million times.

The answer was always the same.

Him.

I closed my eyes as I rinsed the sudsy shampoo out of my water-drenched locks. It was easy to blame someone else for the choices I'd made, but I knew deep down I was more responsible than anyone for being where I was today.

It wasn't a good feeling, to know I'd done so many things wrong, to think of myself as a weak and naïve person.

Not anymore.

I might have made a couple wrong turns on the road of life, but I was pulling a u-ey and heading in the direction I really wanted to go.

I had this apartment with Harlow, a place of our own. It was in a good complex, the neighbors weren't drug addicts, and the streets weren't full of people looking to score. Harlow was a real friend, not just someone who wanted something.

I might still be a stripper, but the truth was I wouldn't be able to make the kind of money I made on a nightly basis doing anything else. I wasn't going to have to strip forever. Soon, I would have more than enough money saved for the program at the technical college I'd been researching. Soon, the only man who would see me without my clothes would be a man I would choose.

Not that I was going to be choosing any man in the next century.

I needed a man like I needed a third nipple.

Which was not at all.

I turned around, letting the full spray of the water hit my shoulders and chest. It felt good, like a gentle warm massage, and I groaned, letting the water pound away some of the soreness in my muscles.

I'd been working some extra shifts at the club, dancing and hefting trays of drinks more often. Lately, I felt this inner sense of urgency, something inside whispering that I needed to move on, that it was time for a change.

But before I could change, I needed enough money to pay for at least a couple semesters at school. I was getting there, and soon I would be able to quit.

A little pang of sadness hit me as I reached for my loofah and body wash. True, I didn't like stripping. And true, I didn't want or need a man.

What about Adam? the naughty voice inside me taunted.

I might have a negative stance on getting involved with men these days, but it seemed he was the exception to that rule. However, just because I might have a small crush on him didn't mean I had to act on it.

Adam was the owner of the Mad Hatter, and that made him my boss. And him being my boss wasn't the only reason he was off-limits. I had several reasons for that.

But it wasn't those reasons that were clouding my mind right now. No, what was clouding my thoughts was the image of his wide shoulders filling out a dress shirt. The way he spoke gruffly to everyone, trying to hide the soft spot I knew he had just beneath his ribs.

I dragged the loofah down over my hip and across my thigh, imagining what it would be like for him to touch me there. For one long moment, I let myself wonder if his fingers would glide over my skin as readily as this soap.

I wasn't a virgin. And yeah, I took my clothes off for money, but locked away in my most private depths was a little piece of the girl I was in high school. The innocent girl who wanted to feel treasured. Who wanted to feel like she was someone's entire world.

Yeah, I knew it was just a schoolgirl's dream.

But it didn't stop me from occasionally letting that part of me out and imagining what it would be like in the arms of a man who loved me more than anything.

That man never used to have a face. He was more of a feeling, more of a dream than anything. But slowly that started to change. Slowly, the man I sometimes longed for became a little clearer in my head.

Sometimes he looked just like Adam.

My eyes shot open and I pulled the loofah away from my body. My skin tingled, and I abruptly turned the water to a shockingly cold temp. I was not going to think about Adam while I washed.

Totally disgusted with myself, I shut off the water and grabbed a towel. My long, deep-brown (the richness in the color courtesy of a box) hair was stick straight no matter how I blow-dried it, so after combing it out, I blasted it with the heat until it hung down my back with the sleekness most women had to pay for with products and blow-outs.

I ran a small flat iron over the straight cut of bangs that were just shy of falling into my eyes and pulled on my panties and a light colored cotton dress. Usually, I wore yoga pants and a T-shirt to work, but it was just too hot today.

I put on the bare minimum of makeup (I would just add more for the stage at work), popped in my violet-colored contacts, and left the bathroom.

Harlow was in the kitchen when I came out, tossing my duffle bag on the end of the sofa. "Hey," I said. "How was work?"

Harlow worked harder than most people I knew. She was determined to achieve her goals no matter how much she had to try. I really admired that about her, and she inspired me to go after what I really wanted in life too.

Harlow shrugged. "It's a job." She made a face, and I laughed.

"The snow cone cart is going to be closing up for the season soon, isn't it?" I asked. She was a snow cone vendor at Broadway at the Beach in addition to waiting tables at the Mad Hatter. She started out stripping, but she hated it, and Adam went against his usual policy that all the girls strip *and* wait tables and let her stay on as a waitress.

She nodded. "Yeah, in just a couple weeks, at the end of October."

October might seem late for the season, but here in Myrtle Beach, it was still warm and tourists were still vacationing.

"Are you going to look for something else?" I asked.

"I don't know yet. With my class schedule, I don't know if I will have time."

Yet another reason I was sticking with stripping. I made a lot of money and the hours were at night, so when I did go to college, I could do both and not have to worry about juggling. I would be sleep-deprived, but it was a small price to pay for bettering my life.

My cell began to ring on the counter. I glanced at it dubiously, making no move to answer it.

"That thing has rung three times since I've been home," Harlow said.

"Sorry." I grabbed it, hit IGNORE, and switched it to vibrate.

"Is he bothering you again, Roxie?" she asked, propping her hip against the counter and turning her full gaze on me.

"He's been trying." I admitted.

I hated talking about Craig. It made me feel like such an idiot, an idiot for letting someone like him dupe me. An idiot for not being strong enough to resist his charm.

"But I've been ignoring him," I added.

"Have you seen him?" Harlow asked, concerned.

"Not since that night at the club."

Several months ago, Craig came into the Mad Hatter, pissed at me because the cops hauled him in for questioning after I was attacked here at home and thought he was responsible. Why he was surprised I would point my finger at him was beyond me. He wasn't nice and he certainly wasn't above using physical force.

'Course, I don't think he was surprised. I think he was just pissed I would actually get him in trouble. Too bad it hadn't been him. I would have loved pressing charges against him and getting him out of my life for good.

The thought caused a funny feeling to erupt deep in my middle. I shoved it away. I knew what it was, and I hated it.

"Do you think he's going to start coming around?" Harlow asked, cutting off my thoughts.

"I don't think so." I hedged. I knew it was only a matter of time. I'd been in this pattern with Craig before. What he didn't know was that I was hell-bent on not repeating my past mistakes.

"Well, at least we know he won't be coming into the Mad Hatter." Harlow pushed away from the counter and walked out into the living room. "Adam will kick his ass."

Adam was not a fan of Craig. A fact he made perfectly clear when Craig showed up at the Mad Hatter and Adam beat him up. The beatdown actually started an all-out brawl in the middle of the club.

I hadn't seen Craig since.

But I knew he was there. Watching. Waiting. Stalking.

He always was.

It made it hard to breathe.

"I was going to stay at Cam's tonight," Harlow said, stepping toward her bedroom. "But I'll call him and tell him to stay here instead."

"No," I said. "There's no reason."

Harlow spun and gave a pointed stare at my cell. I sighed. "He just keeps calling to try and get under my skin. It isn't working. Not this time. It's over. For good. Nothing he can say will change my mind."

"I'm not worried about you going back to him, Rox," Harlow said. "I'm worried what he's going to do when he realizes it."

My stomach turned queasy, but I swallowed down the bile threatening to come up. "He isn't going to do anything. Go to Cam's. Enjoy him. He's one of the good ones. There aren't many of them left."

"If you change your mind, you'll call me?" Harlow asked.

I loved that she didn't press. She didn't try to mother me. I had a mother. I didn't need another one. "I'll call."

She nodded and disappeared into her room. I grabbed my duffle and headed for the door. My eyes instantly scanned the parking lot as soon as I stepped outside.

Paranoia was sticky, just like the storm-laden air. It clung to me with persistence, never allowing me any peace. When I saw nothing out of the ordinary, I made my way to my used Mazda MX-6 and locked the door as soon as I got inside.

He isn't going to do anything. My own words haunted me.

Because deep down, I knew they weren't true.

2

Adam

Dense, sun-warmed sand gave way under the pounding of my running shoes as I jogged along the beach. It was still early in the day, but it was already hot. The air was muggy, and judging by the dark clouds forming over the water, it was probably going to rain at some point today.

If it weren't for the heavy wind blowing off the water, I'd be kicking myself for the punishing pace I had set for myself. But I wanted to get my run in before the rain started falling. The clouds were still far offshore, so I knew I had a while, but it was as good a reason as any to push it hard.

At least if I used this excuse, I wouldn't have to think about the other.

I ran every morning, had been running for so many years it was second nature to me. I was naturally athletic, even if being that way was a lot more work than it used to be. I wasn't going to let that part of myself go. A lot of other things had come and gone in my life, including some of that athleticism, but I was going to hold on to what I could.

My building came into view and I slowed, my body giving a sigh of relief. The familiar twinge of pain in my knee greeted me, but I ignored it. It would probably bother me the rest of the day, and I might even regret the hard workout.

No. Scratch that.

Regrets were for pansies. I was not a pansy. And regretting anything was a waste of time.

After I did some pull-ups and upper body work, I took a shower and got dressed in my usual button-up dress shirt and dark-colored dress pants. Even though I owned a strip club, I still dressed nice. Strip club or not, the Mad Hatter was my business and I was going to treat it as such. Wearing jeans and T-shirts to work (even if they were comfortable) didn't give off the impression I wanted to.

I dealt with suppliers, delivery guys, dancers, customers, etc. on a daily basis. I wanted them all to know I was in charge. Sure, most of that was portrayed through attitude, work ethic, and drive, but I also needed to look the part.

I grinned ruefully at myself for my thoughts. Several years ago, I never would have dreamed this would be my life.

I glanced at the clock. It was still fairly early in the day, so I figured I'd have time to grab some coffee and food on the way into the club. I'd still make it in plenty of time for the phone call I was expecting.

The call was of a more personal nature, and one it seemed like I'd been waiting on for a while. Today was finally the day. The day I would officially be free.

Well, assuming there were no issues that popped up last minute.

God, I hoped not. I was ready to just move on.

And I knew exactly in what direction I wanted to go.

3

Roxie

As soon as I pulled out of the parking lot onto the main road, the sky opened up and rain began pelting my car. And then my gas light came on.

Of course I would need gas in the middle of this monsoon!

I took my chances and drove closer to the Mad Hatter, thinking maybe I would get lucky and the rain would slow down.

It didn't.

So I ended up driving the entire way in the pouring rain, biting my nails and glancing at the gas gauge like every other second. When I got to work, I was sneaking behind the bar and taking a shot. Not that Adam would likely care.

I pulled off the main road and into the lot of the gas station, lucky enough to get a spot at one of the tanks in the center of the roof that covered the pumping area. The rain was thunderous when I climbed out of my old Mazda. After I set it to pumping, I dashed back into the car so I didn't have to stand outside, but the humidity and loudness of the rain was almost intolerable.

When the tank was full, I hopped out and closed the gas cap. A quick glance around told me no one was waiting for my spot so I left my car there and dashed inside to pay. Inside, the smell of coffee captivated me, totally stealing my attention and making my mouth water. Clearly, my taste buds didn't care where the coffee came from so long as it was fresh.

Taking a sharp turn, I yanked a paper cup out of the dispenser and poured it almost full with fresh brew. Then I dumped in about five little cups of vanilla-flavored creamer and gave it a stir. I liked a little coffee with my creamer. Once it was good and mixed I snapped on a black lid, snagged a roll of SweeTarts off a nearby rack, and got in line.

What little sun was allowed to peak through the storm clouds had started to set as I made my way underneath the section of cover back toward my car. I didn't make it very far before a familiar voice stopped me in my tracks.

"Some things never change."

My steps faltered and nervous energy skittered along every single nerve ending in my body. Suddenly, I felt as if I'd just run a marathon, and I had to gasp for breath. Dread was also present. But underneath it all, way down beneath all the many other emotions, was a little bit of eagerness.

I hated it.

I hated that he could make me feel all that. Almost every last feeling he erupted in me was terrible. It hurt. Like physical pain. But then there was this inkling, this tiny little shiver of memory, of what it was like when we first met.

It was like I couldn't shake him.

My fingers tightened around the cup, the heat like a lifeline to sanity. To reality. Slowly, I pivoted around to look at Craig.

"The more things change, the more they stay the same," I replied. He glanced at the coffee and candy in my hand and smirked.

Yeah, I would probably always love coffee and SweeTarts, but I wouldn't always love him.

"How ya been?" he asked like there wasn't all this awful history between us. Like I wasn't going to wear the scars of our relationship forever. He talked almost like we were friends, like the last time I saw him he didn't hurl ugly words and accusations at me. Like he didn't threaten me. Like Adam didn't beat his ass and then he was led away in handcuffs.

I was once duped by that tone of voice. By the way his broad shoulders, lean waist, and baby blues would lean casually against the side of his car. I was totally blinded by the fluttery feeling I got inside my center when he smiled and his wavy dark hair fell into his eyes.

But I knew better now.

I knew bad things could come wrapped in pretty packages.

I knew sometimes charm was just a mask for something darker.

"Better now that you aren't around," I replied, keeping my tone almost nonchalant. The last thing on earth I wanted was for him to see—to even suspect—that he still got to me in any way, shape, or form.

Craig was good at manipulating me.

"I've missed you, baby." He gave no indication he heard my insult. But he had. And it was something I would pay for later if I fell into his sticky trap.

"Surely I'm replaceable," I said and started to turn away. I wasn't the only woman to ever fall for his looks and charm. He'd cheated on me likely from the very beginning. I'd just been too stupid to realize it until I was in way too deep.

I felt his fingers curl around the inside of my elbow just as a loud boom of thunder echoed overhead. The rain was still pelting the cover overhead, and when the wind blew, the sheets of rain slanted and reached for us. My flats were already soaked.

I glanced down to where he held me gently. "Let go."

He did immediately. That was just another one of his ploys. He wanted me to think I was in control, that he would back off when I wanted.

He was a good liar.

"How long you gonna be mad at me, Roxie?" he asked, his voice dipping low. I could feel the heat off his body because he stood so close. Combined with the heat from the air, it was almost suffocating.

"I'm not mad at you, Craig. I'm not anything at all with you." I kept my voice even, bored.

"You're different," he said, recoiling from my words.

I lifted my eyes to his, getting ready for the way he affected me. "I'm not the same seventeen-year-old you once knew. Stop calling me. Stop following me," I said, knowing full well that us "running into" each other was not coincidence. "We're done."

"You've said that before."

"This time I mean it." I walked away without a backward glance. I kept my pace steady, my strides long. If I moved quickly, it was because of the rain, not because I was trying to put distance between us.

My insides were shaking, but I knew I handled that damn well. I was proud of myself. I should be. This time he knew I was serious. He felt the difference behind my words. I saw it in his eyes and I read it off his body. He hadn't expected me to rebuke him this way.

Good.

I unlocked my car and reached for the handle, craving the solitude of the interior. Before I could pull the door open, a rough hand covered mine. He used his body to pin me against the wet metal, his front pressing into my back. He used all his weight, including the eighty pounds he outweighed me by, to keep me from sliding out from beneath him. I had to push back against him, further enhancing our closeness to keep the coffee from being squished against me and the window. I was already wet from the rain; I didn't need to wear my coffee too.

His breath was hot, ruffling my hair as he growled into my ear. "You only get to walk away when I say you can walk away. We aren't done, Roxie. Not by a long shot."

My heart pounded violently against my ribs, and I pushed back, trying to shove him off me. It only made him pin me harder, as if he were trying to remind me who was in control. I sank my teeth into my lower lip against the pain of the door handle gouging into the side of my hip.

Over the hood of my car, I looked for someone to call out to, someone I could make eye contact with.

It amazed me how everyone went along with their own business while Craig stood here and intimidated me this way. It was as if they didn't look, then it wasn't happening.

Cowards.

"The last time you pulled something like this, you ended up bleeding and in handcuffs," I ground out.

"You better not be sleeping with him," Craig growled, his teeth scraping over my ear. "If you are, I will fucking kill him."

Absolute denial and stark fear flooded me at the direct threat to Adam. "I'm not," I said, fervently. Once the words escaped me, I bit my lip harder, until I tasted blood. I shouldn't have said that. Now he knew Adam was important to me.

Craig ground his hips against my backside. A car pulled up at the pump behind mine. "We aren't done yet. You owe me."

I stood there for long moments after he jogged back to his car. After swallowing thickly, I turned my head and looked at the woman now pumping gas just feet away.

Our eyes connected, and then she redirected her gaze somewhere else.

I wrenched my car door open and over the sound of the rain, I heard the sleek purring of an engine. I glanced over the hood of the car to see a cherry-red Mercedes Benz convertible back out of its spot.

Craig was behind the wheel. How had I not noticed the car before?

I'd been too busy making sure he hadn't gotten the best of me.

Yet still he had. He drove off, and I climbed into the driver's seat, abandoning my coffee and candy to the cup holders in the center. After a couple shaky breaths, I drove away.

I had known seeing Craig again was inevitable. It still caught me off guard.

What I hadn't suspected was the expensive car he'd been driving. Craig didn't have money. Holding down a job for more than a month at a time wasn't one of his strong suits.

Not that he had many strong suits.

So, of course, I couldn't help but wonder how the hell he had paid for it.

4

Adam

When the phone in my office finally rang I answered it on the first ring.

"Adam here," I said, gruff. Anticipating this call all frickin' morning was wearing my patience thin.

"Adam, it's Sherman," answered the man on the other end.

"I've been waiting on your call, Sherman."

Sherman was my attorney. After buying the club and having a few marriages fall apart, I figured it would probably be wise to hire an attorney to basically keep on speed dial. I didn't like dealing with the legalities of life, so I paid him to do it for me.

"I'm sorry to keep you waiting. Court ran long this morning."

I rolled my eyes. "Tell me she isn't asking for more shit," I spat.

"She tried, but I managed to get it all dismissed."

I blew out a frustrated breath. "Thanks, Sherman. I really appreciate it."

"She wasn't happy," he said, and I barked a laugh. "That woman was nearly impossible to please… Well, I'm happy to announce that you are officially divorced."

A ten-pound weight lifted off my shoulders. I probably shouldn't feel so relieved that marriage number four was now over. There was also the fact that I had managed to screw up four different marriages, yet I couldn't seem to find any self-loathing.

I was too damn happy to be free.

Of all the wives I had, she was the hardest to divorce. She felt she was entitled to pretty much everything I owned. Unfortunately for her, she wasn't. After my second marriage crumbled, Sherman insisted I get a pre-nup. It wasn't that I was worth millions or anything, but I was comfortable. My business pulled in some money, and I only planned to expand on that.

The business, therefore, most of my money, was mine. She knew she couldn't take any of it if we got divorced. Hell, she signed the papers. That didn't stop her from trying to fight it in divorce court.

Naturally, she was just bitter and angry. I couldn't really blame her.

"So that's it?" I asked Sherman. "Everything is done?"

"Yes, sir. Everything is done."

"Awesome," I said. "Before you go, I wanted to ask you about one other matter."

"Of course," he replied.

"Were you able to extend the restraining order I took out on the asshole?"

"What asshole would that be, sir?" Sherman said dryly.

"Sherman," I said dramatically, "you act like there's a list!"

He snickered on the other end of the line. Then he cleared his throat to answer. "I forgot to mention that. Yes, I was able to get the length of term extended. It's good for another six months."

"You really earned your paycheck today, Sherman!" I told him and grinned into the phone.

After I finished ribbing him, we said our good-byes and I hung up the phone.

Finally. I was divorced. Again.

I wondered if this most current ex of mine was as relieved as I was. I knew I hurt her, and for that I was genuinely sorry. I even let her have more in the divorce than she was entitled. I certainly took my share of the blame for the failed relationships in my past.

And this one, well, it was mostly my fault.

I tried to make it work. But something just kept getting in the way.

Actually, it wasn't a something, but rather a *someone*.

Roxie.

At first, it wasn't that hard to fight the raging hormones she created inside me. She was taken. I was taken. And that was that.

So what if I watched her dances just a little longer than everyone else's? So what if the fact I could bark orders at her and have her sling back some stinging comment secretly thrilled me? I didn't think anyone noticed the slightly favorable way I saw her.

Until my wife came to the club. Apparently, she noticed it right away. I still remember the fight we had that night when she asked me why I never looked at her the way I looked at Roxie. I had no idea what she was talking about. I looked at Roxie the same way I looked at everyone else.

But she didn't think so.

And that woman was like a dog with a bone.

She even demanded I fire Rox.

I put my foot down on that one. There was no way in hell I was firing my best dancer.

And yeah, maybe I'd miss her if I did. But I didn't say that part out loud.

I did everything I could to prove to the wifey that I loved her and no one else. But in all honesty, it was hard to be loyal to one woman when I really wanted to be loyal to someone else.

Even still, I tried. After I heard Roxie was single and had moved in with Harlow, I still tried, even though a voice whispered I might finally have a shot with her.

And then one night changed everything.

Roxie came to work, looking worn out and red in the face. She'd sat in some mechanic's place half the day with no A/C, waiting for the stupid A/C in her car to get fixed.

She looked sick and rundown, so I sent her home. I didn't like seeing her like that; it made my gut feel weird.

But after she was gone, I started worrying that I let her drive home. I wondered if she'd made it and was okay. So I drove to her place to check on her.

I found her attacked, shaking, and the police on their way. Harlow and Cam were there, trying to make sure she was okay. But it wasn't good enough.

I wanted to be the one to take care of her.

I still remember the way she felt in my arms that night. The way her head fit perfectly against my shoulder and the way her silky hair brushed against my jaw. I hated seeing her that way, upset and scared. And when she admitted her ex was abusive… it made me crazy.

I slept on her couch that night, unwilling to leave her place. I needed to be sure she was okay.

I called Sherman the next day and filed for divorce. I told him to get it done as soon as possible.

I couldn't keep trying anymore. Not once I admitted to myself how deep my feelings for Roxie actually ran.

My wife didn't take the news of the divorce very well. She accused me of having an affair with Roxie. It infuriated me for two reasons:

1.) I was a lot of things, but I wasn't a cheat. My second wife cheated on me, and it sucked donkey balls. I'd never do that to someone I made a commitment to. I'd get a divorce first.
and
2.) It was insulting to Roxie, making her out like she was the other woman, a woman I had to hide a relationship with. Roxie was better than that.

Tiff tried to prove I was being unfaithful, but she came up empty every single time. Even though my wife thought I was so low as to actually cheat on her, it didn't make me want to go out and prove her right. That kind of shit was childish.

Instead, out of respect for her, I didn't date at all. I told myself I would wait until everything was finalized before I so much as had a coffee with another woman.

It wasn't easy. Seeing her every day, knowing she was single, and basically rolling the dice that she would stay that way until I could get my shit in order.

Instead of driving myself crazy over the things I couldn't have, I started getting things in place. A plan, if you will. The past several months, I'd been working on something new and it was finally coming together.

All I'd been waiting on was a green light, and Sherman just gave it to me.

5

Roxie

Rain plastered what was left of my dry parts (i.e. my hair), and when I rushed through the door of the Mad Hatter, I was greeted by the rush of the air-conditioner. Usually, it was refreshing. Tonight, it caused goose bumps to race across my skin.

The club wasn't open yet, but the staff was milling around, getting things ready for the crowd that would surely show up. Harlow was off tonight, but Cam was behind the bar, wearing his usual uniform. Black dress pants, no shirt, and a bow tie. On his head was a black fedora that covered his surfer dude blond hair.

I liked Cam a lot. And I figured seeing him behind the bar was a sign.

A sign that I did indeed need a shot.

When I told myself I was taking a shot behind the bar earlier, I hadn't really meant it. And then I had my run-in with Craig. I knew Cam wouldn't say shit, so I figured it was a sign I really did need one.

I dumped my duffle on a nearby barstool and stepped behind the bar. Cam looked up from the glasses he was stacking. "Hey, Roxie."

"Hey."

"Everything okay?" he asked, narrowing his eyes on my face. Most girls probably wouldn't have noticed the narrowed eyes; they'd be too distracted by all the muscle on display, but not me. I didn't check out my best friend's guy. And I tended to look in the places people least suspected. It's how you learned things.

"Not counting the fact the rain ruined my hair?" I said lightly. "I'm good."

Cam grinned. "I need to grab a bottle of Jack out of the back. Watch the bar for me?"

"Of course." I waved him off.

When he was gone, I grabbed the nearest shot glass and the bottle of vodka. I threw it back in one great swallow. It burned going down, and my eyes watered. I wasn't new to drinking, far from it, but doing shots still felt the same.

I felt the alcohol burst into my belly and a gentle fire burned through my middle. Quickly, I dropped the glass into the sink and turned to put the bottle back.

"Roxie!" Adam bellowed. "Get your ass in here!"

I winced. Had he seen?

Quickly, I slid the bottle back home and rushed around the bar to grab my bag. As soon as I slid the strap over my shoulder, I looked up. He was lounging in his office door, watching me.

I felt squirmy, and it was *so* not the vodka.

It was him.

Adam wasn't handsome. He was sexy. He wasn't the kind of guy who took your breath away with his stunning good looks. Adam was the kind of man who took over your thoughts, who owned them. He was the kind of guy who could make a girl like me forget I didn't want a man. He was all alpha male; he exuded strength. He exuded intimidation.

He was gruff, he didn't mince words, and he didn't talk pretty.

But I could see beneath all that. I could see beneath his mask.

Deep down, Adam was a giant softie. I don't even know if he knew it. But I did.

So even when he bellowed my name and stared at me like I was in trouble, I wasn't scared. I don't think I could ever be scared of Adam.

He was wearing khaki dress pants, and even the loose fabric couldn't disguise the thick muscles in his thighs. His white dress shirt was rolled up just below his elbows and open at the throat to reveal a thick neck that gave way to a strong jaw. He had wide cheekbones that slashed across his face, olive-toned skin that always looked tan, wide-set eyes the color of melted chocolate, and dark hair that was buzzed close to his head.

His top lip was shaped like a cupid's bow, and it was currently pulled down in a frown as I walked closer. Adam slid out of the doorway and stepped back, permitting me into his office and shutting the door behind me.

"Hey, I—" I started to apologize immediately. Yeah, this was a strip club, and I was a stripper, but it was still my job. Taking shots behind the bar wasn't professional.

"I want to talk to you," he said, cutting me off.

Wasn't he going to yell at me for the vodka?

"Okay," I said, dropping my bag near the door. The A/C clicked on and a gust of cold air floated down from the ceiling. I suppressed the urge to shiver. It seemed wrong to be so cold when it was so hot outside.

I stepped farther into the room, out from beneath the vent.

Adam leaned over his desk and snagged something off the back of his chair. He turned back and stared at me. "You look like a drowned cat."

"It's raining," I snapped.

Briefly, his eyes traveled over my body, and I became very aware that my light-colored sundress was probably see-through from the rain and that my nipples were painfully hard from the cold.

Instead of leering at me like every other man would and did, his eyes snapped back up to my face and he stepped closer. Automatically, I inhaled, just as I always did when he was close. His scent was intoxicating. It was by far my favorite. Sort of woodsy, deep with a hint of spice. It lingered in my nose even after I breathed out.

The warmth from his large frame radiated around me as he shook out what he was holding and draped it around my shoulders. I glanced down, taken by surprise. I'd been too busy being distracted by his closeness to notice what he was doing.

"You're gonna freeze, Rox," he murmured as he wrapped his jacket around me. "C'mon, slip your arms through."

I did so automatically, hoping his scent would stick to my skin and linger there the rest of the night.

It was ridiculously large, the jacket on my frame. The fabric engulfed me, falling well past my fingers, down my legs, and hanging off my shoulders. Adam grunted and pulled it closer around me. "I didn't realize you were so small," he murmured.

"That's because I have a big mouth."

He chuckled. "Ain't that the truth?"

He pulled away. I was slightly disappointed. Turns out I didn't need vodka. Just the sound of his laugh. The door yanked open with force. Adam was silent maybe two seconds. Then he began issuing orders.

"Amber! Take Roxie's first dance," he barked.

"No," I protested behind him.

He ignored me.

"I need a towel, Cam. A big one." He kept right on yelling.

The door shut once more.

"What the hell, Adam?" I said. "I can do my own dances."

"Relax. I'll cover whatever money you lose. I wanna talk to you."

I huffed and crossed my arms over my chest. It was hard to be annoyed when his jacket was so warm. "So talk."

The door to the office opened, and Cam stuck in his head. He held up the towel, and Adam motioned for it. Cam threw it inside, and he snatched it out of the air.

Cam left us alone again.

"Here," Adam said, letting the towel fall open. He held it out, and as I moved to take it, he changed course and used the corner of the fabric to brush beneath my lip.

"You wanna explain to me why your lip is bleeding?" he asked, shifting closer.

"I bit it," I replied, not offering more of an explanation.

"Why are you so wet?"

"It's raining."

He gave me a no-shit look and lifted his eyebrow, prompting me for a better explanation.

"I had to get gas."

He sighed. "Here."

I took the towel and began to dry my dripping hair.

Adam went back around his desk and sat in his chair. I often thought of it as the king's chair, because Adam was definitely the king of the Mad Hatter.

Once my hair was towel-dried, I slipped off my soaked flats and kicked them aside. My feet were sopping, so I dried them and the rest of my legs. My arms and upper body were warm thanks to Adam's jacket, so I hung the towel over the back of the chair on this side of the desk and pulled my brush from my bag.

I sat in the chair with the towel and began combing out the mess on my head. "What do you want to talk to me about?" I asked curiously.

If it wasn't about the vodka, I had no idea. I knew I was doing a good job here. He couldn't possibly have any complaints.

He watched me for long moments, his eyes following my movements as I brushed. The air was thick in the small office. I could feel his stare, and I tried desperately not to look back, but it was hard. My eyes automatically wanted to look at him, but I was afraid to. I was afraid he would see what I really felt about him in this moment. I was wet, cold, and wearing his jacket. I felt vulnerable and needed a few moments to gather myself.

The vodka needs to hurry the hell up.

When my hair was tangle free, I set the brush in my lap and pulled the damp strands up into a topknot on the crown of my head. I secured it with a hair band from the handle of my brush. When I had nothing left to distract myself, I glanced up at him.

"Your lip still has blood on it," he murmured, like the sight of it bothered him. I ducked my head and dabbed at the sore spot.

When I was done, I lifted my head. "Better?"

He didn't say a word. Instead, he got up and came around the desk, sliding himself between the furniture and me. He crouched down in front of my chair, gently taking the towel from my clutches, and lifted a corner of it to my mouth. Adam was tender as he swiped at the place I had chewed raw. The area stung mildly, but I ignored it as I watched him.

All his attention was directed at that one spot. He concentrated on it as if it were some important test. When he was satisfied, the towel fell from his hand and into my lap. But he didn't pull away. Instead, he brought up the pad of his thumb to softly caress the area, trailing his fingers far past the hurt and across my jaw.

"I don't like seeing you bleed," he whispered.

"It's no big deal," I whispered back.

His hand fell away from my face, and I felt the absence of his touch profoundly. I shivered lightly, and Adam pulled the lapels of his jacket around me just a little bit tighter. His hands lingered in the folds of the fabric. I could feel the heat of them even through the jacket.

Nameless emotion sizzled, crackling through the silence and making me feel buzzed. Maybe the vodka was working after all. Adam wasn't much of a toucher; he usually kept within the bounds of his personal space, very few times venturing out of it.

He was a very controlled man, like he lived by some unspoken personal code. One of his rules was he didn't date his dancers. Ever. And that little reminder was like ice water tossed on the flames he ignited just by being so close.

The tenderness he was showing me right now was just like the tenderness he showed a couple months ago, when he held me in his lap. When his words were soft and meant only for my ears. That night had been horrible. I should never want to think about it.

But I thought about it all the time.

Mostly in the dark of the night when I was lying in bed alone and all I could do was remember.

One night our place was broken into. I was attacked, scared out of my mind. The guy ran off when Harlow showed up, but it didn't really ease my fear. I'd been afraid at the time it was Craig. We knew now it wasn't.

Adam showed up that night. Like he somehow knew I needed him. Just the feel of his arms around me was enough to erase the worst parts of that night and replace them with longing thoughts of him. He spent that night on my couch. I slept better just knowing he was there.

I must have looked now like I looked that night. Maybe it was the reason he was so close.

"You know you can talk to me, right?" he asked, low.

I nodded. I couldn't really, though. My problems weren't his problems. My bad choices weren't his responsibility. And besides, he already knew more than enough about the kind of relationship I'd let myself become involved in. It was embarrassing enough without talking about it more.

"You aren't going to." He said the words like they tasted foul. Momentarily, his hands tightened on the lapels of his jacket before he released them and stood.

"There's nothing to say," I replied.

"I'm opening a new club," he said, abruptly changing the subject. That softness buried deep within him went back where he kept it, and his normal façade came out.

"Congratulations," I said. "Where?"

"The other end of Myrtle Beach." He sat in his chair. "Mad Hatter II, it will be just like this place."

"I'm sure it will be very successful," I said, and I meant it. Adam was a good businessman. He knew how to bring in business and how to keep it. I had no doubt this place made him a lot of money.

"I'm going to be spending a lot of time at the new club in the next couple months, getting it open, training the staff, and making sure it runs as smooth as this place."

"Okay," I said, not sure why he was telling me all this.

"I need someone to manage this place while I'm doing that. I don't want business here to suffer because I'm not always around like I am now."

A little part of me was let down at the prospect of not seeing him every night I was here. Without really even trying, he'd become a constant in my life. Even if I only saw him from across the room on busy nights or from the pole on the stage, I liked knowing he was around.

And now he would be around less.

"Roxie," he said, calling me back to the conversation.

"Sorry," I muttered. "Yeah?"

"I want you to manage this place when I'm not here."

"Me!" I shrieked.

"Yeah." His lip curled up like he was amused. "You."

I was shocked to say the least. Never in a million years would I think he was going to offer me something like this. "I'm just a stripper," I said.

"You are not," he growled. His angry tone made me look up. He was scowling at me darkly. "Sometimes I wonder how the hell you even ended up here," he muttered to himself, but I still heard him.

The words caused a pang of something close to embarrassment to flash through my center. Here wasn't where I thought I'd be. Not in a million years.

"Insulting me isn't going to make me want the job," I snapped.

"It was a compliment," he snapped back.

I laughed.

"Fuck," he muttered and scrubbed a hand over his face. "You know this place inside and out. You've been here longer than any of the other girls, you know how to handle the crowd, the bar, and I know damn well there's a big brain beneath all that," he said, motioning toward my body.

A big brain? Did he seriously just say that?

"I don't hear your customers complaining about all this," I said, motioning to myself.

He slapped his palm on the desktop, making a loud smacking sound. I jumped like a weenie. "Dammit, Roxie," he rumbled. "Quit acting like I'm insulting you."

I stared at him in stony silence.

He blew out a breath. "I meant you're the whole package. Looks *and* brains."

I wanted to tease him further. A million comebacks danced on my tongue. But I held them back. His cheekbones were turning pink, and I found it extremely charming that he was trying so hard to compliment me yet still failing so miserably.

"Thank you, Adam," I said, muffling a smile.

He grunted.

"Can I still dance?" I asked. "If I take your offer?"

"No," he said darkly.

It caught me off guard. I didn't expect such a stark denial.

"Well, why not?"

"Because you're going to be busy managing."

I sighed. As much as I loved the idea of not stripping anymore and taking on a better job here, I couldn't. "I can't."

"What the hell do you mean you can't?" he bellowed.

"I need the money." No other profession made me as much as stripping. It seemed a little ironic that the thing I wanted away from was the thing I had to hold on to just to get away.

I think I just confused myself.

"The job comes with a raise. A good one," Adam said, breaking into my confusion.

A raise was enticing; it made it even harder to say no. Even still, it likely didn't pay as much as I would make on the pole.

I started to shake my head, but a stubborn look crossed his face and he held up his hand. "You're fired."

"What!" I yelled and burst out of my chair. The towel and brush fell onto the tile floor with a clatter. "You can't fire me!"

"The hell I can't!" he argued, also jumping to his feet.

"Oh yeah!" I said. "On what grounds?"

"You're a pain in my ass!" he yelled.

"Well, you're a pain in mine!" I yelled back. I gave a huff and crossed my arms. "You can't fire me because I'm a pain in the ass." I resisted the urge to stick out my tongue.

"How about drinking on the job?" he said quietly.

Shit. He saw.

I sank down in the chair. "I need this job, Adam."

"Fucking A," Adam swore. His cursing was laced with regret, and he pinched the bridge of his nose with his thumb and forefinger. "I'm trying to give you a better job."

"You think I like stripping?" I asked. "You think I don't wanna take your offer?"

"Then why don't you?" He came around the desk again to stare down at me.

"It's my ticket out."

"Your ticket out of what?" he asked. I could tell he was slightly surprised.

"Forget it," I muttered and stood.

Adam snatched my hand and pulled me around, into his personal space. He sat on the edge of his desk and pulled me between his knees.

I could feel the heat of his thighs against my hips.

His personal space was very… *personal.* Very delicious.

"Your ticket out of what, Rox?" he asked again.

I looked up into his molten eyes. "Out of this life. To something better. To college."

He rubbed his thumb across my knuckles as he listened to my words. "College, huh?"

I nodded.

"What you wanna study?"

I glanced away. I don't know why I felt so embarrassed around him. Adam let go of my hand and put his fingers beneath my chin, lifting my face so he could look at me.

"I want to be a nurse," I said.

"Well, that beautiful face of yours sure would distract people from pain."

My breath caught because of his closeness, because of the sincerity in his tone. "That was a pretty good compliment." I smiled.

"Why were you taking shots behind the bar tonight?" he asked, low, his tone gentle and non-accusatory.

"It was only one." I corrected. I lifted a shoulder. "Bad day."

"You know I'm not gonna fire you." His thumb was back to stroking just below my lower lip.

I nodded. I knew.

"Five hundred a night." He tossed the number out there like it was change.

I caught my breath. That was a lot for a management position. Yeah, I might make a little more a week dancing, especially on busy nights, but if I worked six nights a week, that would be three grand.

"How many nights?" I asked.

"As many as you want." He dropped his hand, and I swear for a moment I thought he was going to curl his palm around my hip. My body anticipated it, so when his hand returned to his lap, I was starkly disappointed.

"Okay." I agreed. It was good money, and I wouldn't have to take off my clothes anymore.

"Yeah?" He grinned, lopsided and boyish. My heart totally melted.

I nodded. "Like you gave me a choice," I teased.

"Hey." He caught me around the elbow, drawing my attention. "You always have a choice with me. You know that, right?"

"Yeah," I said, soft. "I know." And I did. He might have threatened to fire me to get his way, but if I really didn't want the job, he wouldn't have turned me out.

I started to take off his jacket. I was warm and mostly dry by that point. He shook his head. "Leave it."

"But it's yours."

"You can use it as an umbrella tonight on the way to your car."

I didn't point out it might not be raining later. The idea of having something of his was just entirely too enticing.

"So when do I start?" I asked, leaving the jacket on.

"Now."

"But I'm on the schedule to dance tonight."

He shrugged.

"Me not dancing tonight would be bad business, and you know it." I pointed out.

A muscle in the side of his jaw ticked. "Fine, but get the girls to cover the rest of the week. Tonight's your last night on the stage."

"Okay," I said, grabbing up my stuff to go in the back and change. I needed to make all I could tonight.

He didn't say anything else as I left his office, but I felt his eyes follow me as I went. I didn't think about his stare because I was too busy thinking about his actions. Why all of the sudden did it seem Adam didn't want me to dance anymore?

6

Adam

I couldn't decide what was harder to look at:
Roxie looking shaken and soaking wet with blood on
her face, or Roxie being engulfed by my jacket.

Both sights were practically impossible to see, for
very different reasons.

When she rushed into the Mad Hatter tonight,
my eyes went right to her. I always knew when Roxie
was around. I felt her before I ever saw her. It didn't
matter if we were in the same room or not, her
presence was never lost on me.

It wasn't every night she came in looking like
she'd fallen out of a boat in the middle the sea. Her
hair was wet and tangled, her clothes saturated and
plastered to her lithe frame, and her shoes were
soaked through.

At first I thought it might be kind of cute, until
she went for the vodka. Roxie didn't drink on the job;
she was the most professional stripper I'd ever had in
this club. So when she retrieved the vodka and
downed it without a second thought, I knew
something was wrong.

And then I saw the blood on her lip.

It made me pissed and suspicious. I knew her ex was a loser, and my stomach tightened to think maybe he'd gotten hold of her again. But I knew better. I knew Roxie wasn't back with him. I paid attention to her, more than she realized.

And yeah, maybe I checked with Harlow every once in a while.

I wished there was more I could do, but if she insisted it was only an accident, I would take her at her word.

For now.

As soon as I banked the raging protective instincts she always brought out in me, I noticed how see-through her saturated dress was. I noticed the hard pebbles in the middle of her fucking perfect tits. How was a man supposed to keep control of the brain in his head and in his pants when she was walking around looking like that?

The misery in her eyes was my control. She was clearly having a rough night, and she was freezing. Covering her up with my coat would not only save my cock from embarrassing me, but also give her some comfort.

Too bad she looked just as sexy drowning in my clothes as she did standing there wet.

Beautiful women were part of my job. Mostly naked, gyrating women were something I saw every single night in this club. In my twenty-five years, I'd seen a lot of hot bodies and sexy females. Hell, I'd been married to four of them.

But it didn't matter because not one of those women knew how to hold my attention.

Except Roxie.

From the minute I first saw her walk into the Mad Hatter looking for a job, I knew there was something different about her. Something that no other woman I'd met had.

I still didn't know exactly what that something was, and it didn't matter. Even unidentified, she still completely captivated me.

But I didn't date my dancers. Ever.

And at the time, I had been married to wife number two. Then three. Then four.

I'd known she'd had a boyfriend, but never gave him much thought, until the whispers started going around backstage. Whispers that eventually trickled into my office.

Roxie was getting knocked around.

Roxie was under some controlling asshole's thumb.

I'd asked her about it once, a long, long time ago. She laughed it off and asked me if I believed everything I heard in a bar.

I should have known she was lying.

For over a year, she was getting beaten right under my nose. Just the knowledge, the thought, of that made me so angry it actually scared me. It was the kind of rage that could lead to murder.

I still didn't know how bad it was. I never felt like I could ask. I felt like it was crossing a line that had been drawn in the sand.

It had taken everything inside me tonight to keep from pulling her against me and kissing every last drop of blood off her lip. I'd imagined way more times than I could count what it would be like to reach up under her clothes, across the silky smooth-looking skin on the back of her thigh, and feel her tremble beneath my touch. Next time she trembled in my arms, it wouldn't be because she was scared.

One day it was going to happen.

One day soon.

The opening of my second club was the perfect excuse to get her off the stage. If I had to listen to one more catcall or see one more leer in her direction from the drunks in this bar, I was going to do something I'd regret.

The thought of anyone looking at her, of putting his hands on her, made me crazy.

This is exactly why I didn't date my dancers.

But I wasn't dating Roxie.

Apparently, that didn't matter.

After tonight, she'd be done with that stage. She'd be clothed and sitting in this office and doing a damn good job of managing this club. I'd meant what I said; she was more than a pretty face. She would run this place almost as good as I did.

And more importantly, she would be safe here. I already saw to that with the restraining order. If her ex even stepped into this parking lot, I'd see his ass in jail. Months ago, he came in here looking for a fight with Roxie. Well, he got one.

Just not with her.

With me.

I made sure that fucker threw the first punch. Then I pounded him in the ground and slapped a restraining order on him so he couldn't come near this property.

I sat at my desk and propped my feet up on the wooden top. After all the time I spent fighting how I felt about her, trying to come up with a way to keep her safe and off that stage, I was finally getting somewhere.

Roxie might not know it yet, but she would very soon.

I was done giving her space.

 7

Roxie

Sexual tension coated my skin. It wound up around my legs like tall grass in the summer. It coated the inside of my mouth, making my tongue restless and needy.

It was a strange feeling. One that was next to impossible to brush off.

Maybe it was odd to be so shaken by the feeling. I was, after all, in the middle of a strip club. And I was walking around barely dressed while drunken men stared their fill. But even here in the Mad Hatter, a bar that made its profit off sex, sexual tension never felt like this.

This was different.

Tonight, the charge in the air wasn't from men looking for cheap thrills. It wasn't from the women gyrating on the stage up front. It wasn't from the scantily clad ladies carrying trays through the crowd. All of those things were external. All of those things happened on a nightly basis. I barely registered them anymore.

So what was it I was registering?

What was it that made me feel like my skin was humming from the inside out? What made me wrap my thighs extra tight around the pole during my last dance and press my core into the hard metal just a little bit more forcefully?

After I set down the last of the beers from my tray, I gave the men a lazy smile and then turned away, giving them a nice view of my behind. It was good for tips.

My strutting faltered, and I gripped the round tray just a little bit tighter when I noted who was watching me. Adam was leaning against the bar, his stance casual, as if he were just checking out the crowd, watching the girls to make sure they were doing what they were supposed to be doing.

But his eyes… His eyes told another story.

From this far away, the chocolate color looked more midnight. His stare was intense, and it wasn't directed at the crowd. It was trained on me. He stared at me as if I were his prey, as if he were lying in wait for the perfect time to strike.

Little ripples of awareness shot up my back as I forced myself to walk through the crowd, trying to pretend I didn't notice the way his eyes were eating me up. I tried to pretend the sexual tension I'd been feeling hadn't just doubled.

I couldn't say I'd never felt intensely attracted to Adam, because I totally was. From the minute I first laid eyes on him coming out of his office and striding his powerful body across the floor to meet me, I wanted him.

Of course, I never did a thing about it, but that was something that seemed to grow more and more difficult every day. Especially when he showed me his tender side (like earlier in his office) and when he stared at me this way.

Something between us felt different tonight, like the tightly honed control Adam always seemed to have around me was unraveling.

Instead of taking my next order around to the end of the bar like I usually did, I slid up next to Adam and called out the order to Cam. After I set the tray on the bar top behind me, I turned, resting both elbows on the counter and leaning against the wood.

"You done dancing?" he said, turning so only one of his elbows was on the bar top and he was facing me.

I shook my head. "One more." One last dance. When I drove to work tonight, I never imagined this would be the final night I'd strip in the Mad Hatter.

He grunted, which wasn't really an answer, but it still left me wondering once more why it seemed he didn't want me to dance anymore.

"You know, if my dancing sucks, you could just tell me," I said, point blank.

He shifted closer and his entire front almost brushed against my body as he leaned down to talk quietly in my ear. "What makes you think I don't like your dancing?" It was a simple sentence, a question. But the way he spoke low, so it only reached my ear, the way he sort of leaned in to my body and his warmth and scent wrapped around me… I realized.

I realized the humming just beneath my skin, the restless way I danced earlier, the tension that seemed to coil just beneath my ribcage… it was him.

The sexual tension that flooded me tonight was from Adam.

Holding my body still even though I desperately wanted to lean closer, I tipped my head back and stared up at him. The rich shade of his eyes speared me, and my breath faltered. "Because," I said, wetting my lips with my tongue, "you seem in an awful big hurry to get me off that stage."

His eyes dropped down to my mouth, igniting a slow burn in my center. "Maybe I'm just tired of you dancing for other men," he rumbled.

The bottom fell out of my stomach. Thank goodness I was leaning against the bar because surprise so strong flickered through me that I was unable to feel anything else.

Did he just imply he wanted me to dance for him?

"I didn't know it bothered you," I said, turning so my posture mirrored his. Now we were facing each other, both of us with one elbow propped on the bar.

"Now you do," he said and he leaned closer, a little bit of challenge in his dark eyes. "What are you going to do about it?"

I never backed down from a challenge.

I straightened off the bar and stepped closer, my chest brushing up against his as I reached out and gripped the collar of his white dress shirt, adjusting it near his throat. There wasn't anything about it that needed fixing; I just wanted to touch him.

His eyes narrowed slightly as he watched me. "Guess you'll have to wait and see," I murmured, smoothing my palms across his broad shoulders and then stepping away.

One of the girls motioned it was my almost my time for the stage, so I motioned to the tray of drinks and yelled out the table number so she could deliver the booze. Adam was still watching me. The air around us still crackled and the humming beneath my skin graduated to a vibration.

Without another word, I walked away, stopping off in his office on my way backstage. I knew exactly what I was after and where he kept it. Once my hand closed around the silk, I stuffed it in my apron and rushed backstage.

As the girl on stage finished up her dance, I changed quickly, bypassing the outfit I planned to wear and going in a completely different direction instead.

I dug into the bottom of my duffle for the panties I didn't usually wear for dancing. I only had them to change into after I was done my shift tonight. They weren't lacey thongs or tiny-cut bikinis like I usually danced in. These were soft cotton boy shorts. They hugged my ass and the very top of my thigh. The low-cut waistband was made of lace, and it curved well below my belly button, exposing all of my flat navel. They were deep black, and on the very front there was a ruching detail that gathered the fabric, exposing even more leg, punctuated on each side with a small hot-pink satin bow.

Frankly, these were more comfortable than anything I ever wore on stage, and they made me feel far sexier than any of the tiny outfits I usually wore. I liked them because when I walked around in public, I always felt like I was carrying a naughty secret because no one knew the sexiness I was hiding beneath my clothes.

I slipped them on and pulled off my top. I didn't bother with a bra. Instead, I grabbed up the suit jacket that Adam pulled around me and slid it over my bare skin. The inside had a silky liner and it glided right over my touch-sensitive body.

After that, I stepped into a pair of black sky-high stiletto heels, pulled my hair down from the bun it was in and let the messy, tangled strands fall over my shoulders and around my face. Some of the strands were still damp from the rain, and I scrunched them up, trying to infuse even more body.

Just as the music onstage was ending, I yanked out the stolen item from Adam's office and slid it over my head—the tie he kept for meetings. I adjusted the blue silk, letting it drape around my neck as I fixed the knot and made it so the fabric fell just between my bare breasts.

I noticed some of the girls staring at me from the corners of their eyes as I added some fuchsia lipstick and ruffled up my hair one last time.

"That's a new look for you." One of the dancers spoke up.

"Yep," I replied, stepping up behind the curtain. "Figured I would end my dancing career with a bang."

Butterflies took flight in my middle, and I moved restlessly against the silk hanging in the center of my breasts. Having his clothes, things he wore on his body, brushing against my naked skin excited me. I'd never been so keyed up, so turned on for a dance before.

Adam said he didn't like me dancing for other men.

So this time, I was going to dance just for him.

8

Adam

I was going over an inventory sheet behind the bar, checking it against the supply of liquor, when the music came on. It wasn't anything special, just the usual instrumental style with a slow-paced, heavy beat that made every man in the place think of sex.

The room was dim, most everything cast in shadows except the area right around the bar. A single spotlight shone down in the center of the stage, drawing everyone's eye.

I only glanced up and then didn't look up again.

Until a hushed sort of murmuring seemed to race over the people sitting around the stage. I looked up from my notes. The stage was still empty; the light illuminated nothing at all. The grinding rhythm of the music filled the space as men looked around, wondering where the hell the entertainment was.

Wasn't Roxie supposed to be up?

What the hell was she dragging this out for? She needed to get on stage, shake her ass, and be done. I wasn't kidding when I told her I was done watching her shake it for other men.

I began to feel suspicious, remembering how her tight, round ass bounced into my office before disappearing backstage. What the hell was she up to now?

I was just about to abandon the inventory to go see what was going on when a catcall echoed through the bar. As soon as it ended, a few whistles and shouts immediately followed. I glanced back at the stage.

Roxie was there, standing just out of the circle of light but with her leg partially stepped inside. The only thing anyone could make out of her shape was her sleek, slim calf and sexy-as-hell black heels.

She rolled her foot around, flexing the creamy smoothness of her leg, and as more whistles cut through the music, she stepped all the way beneath the spotlight.

The clipboard I held fell out of my hands, landing with a thump on the top of the bar. The inside of my mouth suddenly went dry, as if I'd been walking through a desert in the dead heat of day.

Roxie was wearing my jacket. Her long, bare legs stuck out from beneath it and stretched all the way to the floor. It hung off her frame, too large to mold against her, but it didn't matter. Just imagining what was beneath it was sexy enough.

She shook out the mess of dark hair tumbling over her shoulders and bent. Roxie dragged her fingers up her bare leg and arched her back as she straightened, giving every single eye in the place a glimpse of her tight black panties, pink bows, and bare waist.

Her hand stopped just shy of revealing her chest, and she slid her fingers over and glided them up and down a tie hanging around her neck. My cock tightened watching the pumping action.

Men in the audience were hooting and hollering, but I barely heard them. My hearing seemed to go out…

That was *my* tie.

She was wearing my jacket and my tie.

My blood pressure spiked and the room tilted. Desire unlike anything I'd ever felt before hounded me, so strong I had to grip the edge of the bar for support.

Roxie shimmied around and then spun, putting her back to the crowd. Very slowly, the jacket began to slide down. Inch by beautiful inch, the smooth skin of her back was revealed. Lower and lower the fabric drooped until it was painfully obvious she wasn't wearing a bra.

Abruptly, she spun, clutching the jacket around her waist, baring her shoulders and giving insanely provocative peeks of her bare breasts. It was impossible to see all of them because her hair covered them, and the tie… the fucking silk tie slid right between the perky globes.

My dick began to stir in my trousers, throbbing almost painfully, and I shifted so I was standing that much closer to the bar so it concealed my obvious desire.

Roxie slid the jacket back up as various men yelled for her to take it off, and even as I wanted to pound every single one of these assholes for looking at her, part of me also begged her to drop it.

She began moving around more, dancing, shimmying, and teasing. She rocked the pole toward the end of the stage like no one else. Her upper body strength was incredible, and the way her thighs hugged the metal as she practically dry-humped the pole made me almost bust a nut in my pants. Through it all, the jacket fell lower and lower off her shoulders.

Roxie shimmied her fine ass all the way to the top of the pole and then stopped. Holding herself there, she took off the jacket completely and let it float to the floor.

The men in the place went crazy, but I could only stare. Slowly, seductively, she slid down the pole with grace no one else seemed to understand, and then she stood, sliding her hands over the tie around her neck, her eyes connected with mine.

The corner of her full, pink lips curved up, and she blew me a kiss.

Everyone else in the entire bar fell away. Her eyes never left me as she danced, shook, and touched herself.

I'd never before gotten so hard without a single touch in my entire life.

I don't know how long she danced. I couldn't even tell you how long the music played. My entire world seemed to shrink down to only her and her movements. Her and my tie.

If I had any doubt about now being the time to let her know how I felt about her, it was completely erased with that dance.

I wanted Roxie. I was going to have her. She was practically inviting me into her hot, tight body right now.

I was still under her spell, barely even able to breathe, when I felt Cam's hand slap my shoulder.

"Might wanna wipe that look off your face there, boss," he said, amused.

I stiffened and blinked. Roxie was pulling on my jacket and money flooded the stage around her heels.

"Jesus," I muttered.

Cam chuckled. "If that dance wasn't a message, then I don't know what was."

I tore my gaze away from Roxie and looked at him. "What are you saying?" I half growled as I blinked. It seemed the rest of the world didn't want to come back into focus.

"I'm saying I think it's about time you and Roxie do something about all that tension between you."

"Cover the bar," I told him. I didn't really have to remind him to do his job, but those were the only words I could push past my tongue. I adjusted my hard-as-steel junk and then gave up. Everyone who looked was going to get a damn eyeful because there was no hiding how fucking hard I was.

On my way to my office, Roxie was stepping off the stage, a few drunken assholes salivating at the bottom of the stairs, waiting for her to arrive.

Anger and extreme possessiveness rushed over me, and I shoved my way through the group, practically snarling for them to step back. Roxie's eyes widened when she saw me, and I reached out and snatched her hand, gripping it tightly in mine, and towed her toward my office.

The entire wall shook with the force in which I slammed the door.

Roxie stood there, her cheeks flushed, her lips stained pink, and her hair a mess. Her violet eyes were round and slightly wary as she stared at me. I blew out a breath and took in the jacket, tie, and heels.

"You danced for me," I said, the words ripping from my throat.

"Just for you," she said softly.

A half growl, half moan ripped from my throat, and I leapt at her, plowing into her and shoving her back against the wall. I slid my arm beneath her so I was the one who took the force of the shove, and I pinned her with my body. Her chest heaved, and I could feel the rapid beating of her heart.

I wrapped my free hand around the length of the tie. "You stole my tie."

"You can have it back," she purred.

"It looks better on you." I used the tie like a leash and pulled her even closer, towing her until our mouths were just barely inches apart.

Before bringing my lips down on hers, I pushed into her just a little bit farther, tilting my hips upward so the hard rod in my pants could be felt along her front.

She gasped. I smiled. "I hope you're ready for what you just did, sweetheart," I murmured.

Then I crushed my lips to hers.

9

Roxie

I could count on a single hand the number of men I have kissed in my life.

It might have well been zero though, because the minute, *no, the second,* Adam's mouth fused with mine, my past no longer mattered. Every kiss I'd ever thought I enjoyed was proven a lie.

A rush of heat suffused my skin, and I knew if I looked down, I would see a fine pink flush spreading over my skin. Adam's lips were supple and moist, a soft place to fall while he rendered me almost incapacitated. He didn't lift his mouth, not one time. Instead his lips rubbed furiously over mine, creating a sort of friction that crackled in the space around us.

Our lips glided across each other, like they knew exactly how they fit together and the exact moment to shift so the pleasure was intensified. Adam slid both arms around me, crushing me against him. The hardness pressing into my center was almost painful, but it was the kind of pain that made my crotch throb. I wound my arms up around his neck, cupping the base of his head with my palm, and let my tongue dart out across his perfectly seductive lips.

He growled. The action vibrated my chest as he sucked my tongue into his mouth, stroking it and coaxing it deeper until it brushed over the roof of his mouth.

One of his hands slid down the small of my back and over the curve of my ass, where he filled his hand with my flesh and squeezed like he wanted me even closer. I wanted closer too, but there was too much between us.

I ripped my mouth away, gasping for breath, and bit down on my swollen bottom lip. Adam's eyes were unfocused and heavy-lidded as he stared down at me. My pink lipstick marred the perfect shape of his full mouth, and it totally turned me on to see I had marked him in some way.

He swooped down to kiss me again, and when our lips latched together, I reached between us to fumble with the buttons on his dress shirt. I wanted to feel his skin. It seemed like I'd waited forever for him to touch me like this, for a kiss that totally blocked out the rest of the world. I was taking advantage while I had the chance.

Except my hands were shaking and my fingers kept missing their mark. How the hell was I supposed to remove his shirt when his lips were assaulting me to the point I couldn't function?

I made a frustrated sound and he swallowed it down. His chuckle floated between my lips as he pushed my hands away and took matters into his own hands.

Those buttons never stood a chance.

The sound of them scattering across the hardwood on the floor barely registered as he literally ripped the fabric off his chest. I was on him before he even had the shirt totally pulled off his arms.

His chest was like granite, hard and carved, bronzed, and so incredibly smooth. My fingers slid over him like water. The silkiness of his skin made me sink my teeth into his lower lip as if feeling him wasn't enough and I had to taste him too. Holy crap, he was broad. There was so much of him to explore my hands couldn't move fast enough. I loved the way his muscles bunched beneath his skin, the tightness in his form, and the way when he wrapped his arms back around me, it was like he totally surrounded me. I was completely captured by his coppered, oversized body.

He made me feel small, but not in a helpless way. Small in the sense the passion between us was so big it overpowered my frame.

My hands fondled all the way down to the waistband of his pants. My fingertips flirted with the line between skin and clothing. Adam made a sound and ripped his mouth away to stare down with lust-filled eyes.

Abruptly, he spun, taking me with him, pulling me away from the door and walking us over to the desk. Like it was nothing at all, he lifted me by the waist and sat me on the edge of his desk and fit himself between my thighs. With glittering eyes, he looked down at the tie and grasped the lapels of his jacket.

Slowly, he peeled away the fabric, baring my naked chest. The rush of air was shocking because my skin was so incredibly hot. My nipples tightened into hard little knots, and they grew achy as he stared at me.

"I don't want anyone else looking at you again, Rox," he rumbled, oh so gently brushing the backs of his knuckles over the sensitized skin of my breast.

I shivered.

"I could say the same to you," I whispered, tucking some fingers in his waistband.

The force of his body sent me arching over the top of his desk. I would have lain out completely flat, but he slid his arm beneath the small of my back and arched me up so my naked chest was completely flush against his.

I ceased to think. All I knew was the feel of him against me and the seductive kiss that went on and on.

The sexy beat of the music from the stage made me want to grind against him, but I couldn't because of the way I was positioned. Tension coiled inside me so tightly I moved restlessly, and a little helpless sound ripped from my throat.

Adam pulled back but kept his arm around me, supporting my yielding body. "Jesus Christ," he swore, his voice thick and gravely. My lips felt swollen and moist, and as he withdrew even farther, he swiped at my lower lip with his thumb.

He picked up his jacket and draped it around my shoulders. "You gotta put that shit away, Rox. If you don't, I'm going to take you right here on the desk."

I pressed my lips together because if I opened my mouth, I'd likely beg for just that.

He groaned. "Don't look at me like that," he rumbled and rubbed a hand over the top of his head. "I've been waiting too goddamn long for a chance with you. Our first time is not going to be in this office with a bunch of drunk assholes on the other side of the door."

"You've been waiting for me?" I whispered, gripping the front of the jacket.

"Guess I have," he quietly replied. When his eyes brushed over me, the tenderness in his gaze almost made me swoon. He had a way of making a girl feel like she was the only one in the entire world.

I wondered if any of his four wives ever felt like that.

The thought helped break some of the tension inside me. I might want Adam, he might turn me on in ways I never imagined, but getting involved with him probably wasn't a safe bet.

I wanted safe right now. I needed it. The best way for me to have the safety I desperately needed was by remaining alone, by taking care of myself.

"I should get back to work," I said, hopping off the desk. "There's a big crowd out there tonight."

His eyes narrowed slightly at the sudden change in my demeanor. I hoped he didn't press. His kiss, his touch, and that dance left me feeling weak inside. If he pushed me right now, I might cave.

"Can you come in early tomorrow for training? In the afternoon, before the club opens?" he asked. There wasn't a hint of anger in his tone.

I hated to admit it, but I was surprised. I had been expecting him to be angry or to make some kind of comment about how I led him on and then put on the brakes.

But he didn't seem angry at all. He didn't act disappointed in me or let down. It crumbled a little piece of the wall I had built around my heart these last couple of years.

"Sure, I'll be here," I replied. Every step that brought me closer to the door left me feeling regretful. I didn't want to go back out there. I wanted to stay in here, with Adam.

Of course, that was exactly the reason I had to go.

I pushed my arms through the jacket, once again reveling in how it swallowed me up. Abruptly, I spun on my heel, clutching the coat against me. "You can't have this back," I burst out. As soon as the words left my mouth, I felt my eyes widen in surprise.

What the hell? I sounded like a spoiled five-year-old.

He smiled lazily and wandered over in front of me, taking his time prowling closer. My eyes fastened on his chest and the way it moved.

"Sweetheart, I wouldn't dream of taking it back." One of his arms wrapped around my shoulders, pulling me in as he pressed a lingering kiss to my hairline. His mouth was warm and soft; the feel of his lips gave me little shivers along my spine. He didn't lift his head when he spoke, so his breath danced over my forehead and ruffled my hair. "Put some clothes on before you go back out there, sweetheart. I'm feeling extremely possessive tonight."

If words had a flavor, those would have been a giant, warm-from-the-oven donut drizzled in warm, gooey glaze. Sinful, bad for you… but so damn good.

"'Kay." I agreed.

He reached around me and opened the door. The sounds of the bar pressed in on me, intruding upon our little bubble.

"Rox?" he said quietly, but even over the music and rambunctious crowd, I heard him.

I glanced over my shoulder, peeking around my tangled hair.

"Thanks for the dance." The corner of his mouth turned up, an ornery smile stealing over his features.

I winked and walked away.

Backstage, the girls all started clapping when I stepped up to my table. I felt my cheeks flame under the attention. Thankfully, it didn't last very long because we were all busy and had work to do. I grabbed an outfit out of my bag to finish my shift. It was the only outfit of mine that offered some sort of modesty.

With the fabric still clutched in my hand, I sagged against the makeup table and blew out a shaky breath.

I should be congratulating myself for staying strong, for avoiding a situation that would likely end in more heartache.

But I wasn't.

Deep down, I knew I hadn't avoided anything with Adam. I'd just made it even more inevitable.

10

Adam

I had to stay in my office for a while after Roxie went back to work. If I didn't like to wear jeans at work because of professionalism, imagine how unprofessional my boner would be.

I'd never wanted a woman this bad before. Maybe because I'd never tried to fight my attraction to one before. Of course, if that were the case, then wouldn't that kiss have lessened my want? Wouldn't it have sated at least a little part of my desire?

It didn't.

It left me with a serious hard-on, a tent in my pants, and the possibility of blue balls.

Eventually, I was able to focus on something other than the way it felt to finally kiss her, and I credited that to reading the manual for the electric pencil sharpener on my desk.

The club was just about empty when I left my office. The dancers were done for the night, and a few of the girls were finishing up their shifts.

My gaze found Roxie automatically, and I noticed she looked a little strained.

How the hell could she already look like that after the kiss I laid on her? She should still be walking around on wobbly knees!

"Roxie!" I bellowed.

My sudden yell made her jump, and I felt bad. I hadn't meant to scare her.

"Do you have any other volume besides extremely obnoxious?" she asked, coming over to where I stood.

I leaned in close, dropping my gaze to her mouth. "Oh, I think you know I do."

She pressed her lips together like she was remembering the kiss. I was totally the man.

"Why do you look like something is wrong?" I asked, trying my best to not be obnoxious.

She turned her head slightly, her eyes slipping over to where a couple people still sat in the club. "Nothing's wrong," she answered, looking back at me. "Just ready to go home."

I scanned the people still sitting around. A table of guys who looked to be about twenty-one were talking to one of the dancers, a couple sat nestled in the corner, finishing off their drinks, and a lone man hunched over his beer and staring down at his cell phone.

"Are any of the guys bothering you?" I asked, not really seeing anything that might be a problem, but unsure just the same.

"No," she replied quickly. A little too quickly.

"Club's closing!" I called, and everyone started to get ready to go. If someone was bothering her, then they wouldn't be an issue very long.

"Why don't you go ahead and leave for the night?" I told her. "Everything's about done here anyway."

"Are you sure?" she asked.

"Grab your stuff. I'll walk you to your car."

A few minutes later, she came out with a duffle bag in her hand and my jacket slung over her arm. I didn't hesitate to slip the bag off her shoulder and take the jacket from her grasp. Before she could say anything, I held it out so she could slip her arms inside.

Once my coat was around her, I picked up her duffle and guided her to the door. We bypassed the bouncer out into the empty parking lot. She was parked around the side of the building so we headed in that direction.

When we arrived at her car, I was sort of hesitant to let her leave. I felt like I'd been waiting for her forever. I took the keys out of her hand, started up the car for her, and tossed the duffle in the backseat.

When I pulled out of the car, she was standing directly behind me. I shut the driver's door and leaned against it, curling my fingers around the lapels of my jacket and tugging her a little closer.

"I like your lips," I murmured, staring down at the object of my affection.

"Just my lips?" she whispered, a small smile playing over her mouth.

"I might be partial to everything else around them too."

"I might like that." Roxie swayed a little closer, pressing me into the side of the car, and I tightened my hands on the front of the jacket and lowered my head.

Her lips were soft and warm, the kiss was tender, and it was entirely easy to lose myself in the feel of her. The steady rhythm in which we moved together was far better than any song I'd ever heard, and I released the jacket so I could cup her face and pull her closer.

Roxie made a little sound in the back of her throat as her soft lips parted. I slipped my tongue into her mouth and gently teased until she melded against me like it was hard for her to stand.

I forgot we were outside in a parking lot. The way she felt in my arms was most arguably the most incredible thing I'd ever experienced. She was all soft and curvy, her body begging to be explored. My hands slipped into the opening of the jacket and slid across her waist and around to the small of her back.

Roxie's fingers skirted over the exposed skin at my neck and throat, lightly climbing up the side of my jaw and around the back of my head.

The sound of a car door slamming intruded upon our moment, and I drew back slowly, blinking down at her. Roxie's little pink tongue darted out over her bottom lip, capturing what was left of our kiss. It was fucking hot, and I wanted to kiss her again. I wanted to pull off all the fabric between us and rub our bodies together until we both fell over the edge of bliss.

"Thanks for walking me to my car," she whispered, tilting her head back to look up at me.

Her bangs were falling into her eyes, so I brushed them back and smiled. "It was my pleasure."

Reluctantly, I reached around behind us and unlatched the car door. I stood close and she slid into the driver's seat, and because I couldn't *not* touch her one last time, I reached in to buckle the seatbelt around her.

"Drive safe," I whispered and kissed her temple.

She sighed, and my gut tightened.

I watched her car until the taillights disappeared. One of these days, sooner rather than later, I wasn't going to have to watch her drive away. She was going to be with me.

The distinct sound of heels clicking across the pavement broke into the spell Roxie had cast. I watched as someone familiar seemed to materialize out of the shadows along the side of the building.

Parked off to the side was a car I knew all too well, a car I paid for.

"The ink is barely dry on the divorce papers, and here you are, working on wife number five," my ex said bitterly, stopping just several feet in front of me. "Are you going to stand there and deny you want her even after what I just saw?"

Aww fuck.

And tonight had been going so well.

11

Roxie

I could kiss him forever.

It was late. The roads were dark and practically empty as I drove home from the club. Everything was still wet from the heavy rainstorm earlier, but I barely noticed.

I couldn't even worry about the guy who sat in the club tonight, the one whose stare seemed to burn a hole right through my back. All night it was hard to shake the feeling I was being watched. Every time I was out on the floor, taking orders and delivering drinks, the little hairs on the back of my neck would stand tall.

My eyes kept going to the man sitting alone, drinking beer. Every time I glanced his way, he appeared to be engrossed in his cell phone, but I had caught him once. Caught him staring at me, the intensity in his gaze making my skin crawl.

But then he went back to his phone, and I was left wondering if I was just being paranoid.

I'd seen him a couple times at the club, and each time he creeped me out. But he'd never done anything to make me think he was dangerous. In fact, he'd never even spoken to me.

But whatever. The creepy man in the bar was the last thing on my mind because everything in my head paled in comparison to Adam. I couldn't stop reliving the kiss.

The. Kiss.

It played such a prominent role in my head I felt like it needed a title of its own. I had been so keyed up when I left his office that it took the rest of the night just to breathe normally again.

And then he walked me to my car.

And kissed me again.

I should have been scared out of my mind. Scared of my reaction to what happened between us tonight.

I knew better than to get tangled up with a man who would probably only hurt me. True, Adam had never been anything but good to me since I met him, but his track record told a different story.

He'd been married four times. Four. If he would marry and then divorce so easily, then it didn't bode well for any kind of relationship we might have. And sure, if I were in any other kind of place in my life, maybe a casual fling would be okay.

But I wasn't in that frame of mind. Hell, who was I kidding? I never would be. I put everything I had into my relationship with Craig. I made excuses for him, I blamed myself, and I basically tried way too hard to make it work with him even when I should have walked away.

Deep down I was a relationship kind of girl. Deep down I craved that one person who would always be there. That one person who would always love me no matter what.

While my heart whispered—*hoped*—it might be Adam, my brain told me to get real.

It was so hard thinking with my head when my heart was involved.

A pair of headlights bobbed in the rearview mirror, momentarily distracting me. I glanced at the car that seemed to appear out of nowhere.

It was red.

It looked sporty.

I thought about the gas station before work, about Craig and the car I'd seen him drive away in. A funny feeling unfurled in my gut, making my nerve endings sizzle with warning.

It couldn't be.

All thoughts of Adam, our kisses, and my final dance earlier tonight fled my brain. Adrenaline began to flood my system. I knew I shouldn't be scared. I was probably overreacting. But I couldn't help it. I was out alone in the dark, the road was almost empty, and a car that looked suspiciously like the one Craig had been driving was following along behind me.

My hands tightened around the steering wheel, squeezing until it was almost painful. My back stiffened and my legs locked up, squeezing together from the knees up. As I drove, I glanced in the rearview mirror almost obsessively.

The car was just driving along behind me. It wasn't tailing me. It wasn't driving erratically. There was no reason for me to believe I was in danger.

I came to an intersection up ahead. On impulse, I braked and swerved into the left turning lane. This wasn't my road; it wasn't my turn or my neighborhood. But I could go down this road, then loop around and catch this main street again to take me on to my apartment.

My blinker seemed incredibly loud as I made the turn onto the street.

The red car followed.

As it turned, I got a better glimpse at the vehicle. It was a two-seater sports car. The dark shadow of a single driver in the front made my pulse spike.

"Shit," I muttered. "Don't panic," I told myself.

Then I laughed.

I was totally panicking right now.

I went down the street, passing darkened houses and businesses already closed for the night. As I neared the back of a lit-up gas station, I glanced up to see the car still just behind me. It was closer than it had been on the main road. Close enough that if I slammed on my brakes, he would hit me.

Impulsively, I swerved into the parking lot of the gas station, my tires making a loud screeching sound on the pavement. As I furiously spun the steering wheel and pointed my car into the front of the lot, I glanced out the back window.

The red sportster halted completely, having overshot the turn into the lot. The car reversed and then turned to follow me.

Okay. He was totally following me.

I hit the gas, ripping through the lot, a nearby car blaring its horn at me as I sped, but I didn't slow down. Instead, I pulled out in front of an oncoming car and back onto the main street. My place was only minutes away. Maybe if I sped and drove crazy, he would back off.

And if he didn't...

Well, then I'd get pulled over by the cops and that would totally scare him away.

I made it out onto the main road and through a nearby light without any sign of the other car. I breathed a sigh of relief and leaned back into the seat, relaxing just a little. My arms and legs began to shake from the adrenaline that had flooded my body.

Maybe it was just some asshole wanting to scare someone for fun.

I looked up in the rearview mirror again.

The red car was zipping through the light, several car lengths behind me.

I pressed down on the gas pedal, increasing my speed and ripping down the street. Up ahead, the final light before I arrived at my building turned yellow. I sped up even more, refusing to get caught by the red light.

"Come on. Come on," I muttered as I tore down the street, staring at the light, willing it to stay yellow.

Just as I approached it, the light switched from yellow to red. I glanced behind me. The red car was almost caught up.

"Fuck this," I muttered and went through the light.

Just before I turned into the parking lot of my place, I noted the red car sitting down the street at the red light.

How much longer until it turned green?

I wasn't going to wait around to find out. I ripped through the parking lot and prayed there was an open spot near our apartment. I cried out with relief when I saw the vacant spot just up ahead that was right in front of the stairs leading to mine and Harlow's place.

My front tires hit the curb with a jolt when I slid into the spot. I grabbed my keys and bag and burst from the car and slammed the door. After making sure no red car was waiting, I took the stairs two at a time while fumbling with my keys.

The sound of a car engine purring grew closer, and I hopped from one foot to the other as I turned the key in the lock. When I heard the latch click home, I forced myself so hard into the apartment that I stumbled and almost fell.

I recovered quickly, jumped up, and slammed the door. The distinct sound of my keys and keychain banging against the outside of the door made me freak out all over again.

I'd left my keys hanging in the lock!

I took a deep breath and tried to calm my racing heart. I reached for the door handle and turned it, cracking the door once more. The glare of headlights out in the parking lot made me squint as my stomach turned in knots.

I pushed my hand through the crack and pulled the keys inside with me and then slammed it closed.

After I bolted all the locks, I crept over to the window in the living room. The white blinds were closed. Using a single finger I slid one of the slats up just a little and leaned over to look out into the night.

The red car was sitting at the curb.

Horrible memories of the night I was attacked in this apartment assaulted me. I wasn't going through that again. Especially because this time I knew the man outside was here for me.

I didn't know exactly what he wanted, but I had enough experience with him to worry.

The slat fell back into place, and I rushed for my bag, dumping all the contents out onto the floor and fumbling for my cell. I was calling the cops.

Clutching the phone as I called up the emergency number on the screen, I crept back over to the window. I don't know why I moved like I was sneaking. It wasn't like he could see me in here.

Just before I hit SEND, I peeked back outside.

He was driving away. Like a snail, the red car inched its way out of the parking lot and around the corner, out of sight.

Clutching the phone, I collapsed onto the couch. He was gone.

The silence of the room pressed in on me. Suddenly, I was sorry I told Harlow to go stay at Cam's tonight.

I knew I could call her, but really, I didn't want to have the conversation that would go along with that call. Instead, I snuggled down into Adam's jacket, keeping the phone close by, and prepared myself for a very long night.

12

Adam

"What are you doing here, Tiff?" I asked, not in the slightest mood to argue with my newly crowned ex.

"Thought I'd come by and see if your shark of a lawyer told you the divorce was final," she replied. "But I can see you already heard."

I sighed. I was sorry she saw that, but in my defense, I did wait until everything was finalized to act on anything I felt for Roxie. "Sherman isn't a shark and I think you know that," I said, not bothering to respond to her jealousy.

"Why weren't you in court today?" She sniffed.

"I was trying to avoid a conversation like this," I muttered.

"I don't know why I expected more from you," she said. "I should have paid more attention to your track record."

I ran a hand over my head and bit back a nasty reply. I was no saint. Some people might even call me a serial marrier. I couldn't really explain why I'd felt the need to get married so many times. I didn't have a shitty childhood. I wasn't afraid to be alone.

My parents were happily married, still together, and didn't pressure me to find a relationship like they shared.

Maybe I thought marriage was the way to prove I truly cared about a woman. Maybe deep down I was searching for that one person, the one that would complete me.

Or maybe I just liked to be in relationships.

I never really bothered to sit down and analyze my past choices or mistakes. Reliving the past felt sort of like throwing up last night's dinner and eating it again.

"Look, Tiffany," I said, stepping closer to her. She was a beautiful woman. Long blond hair, graceful long limbs, and a sculpted, smooth face.

But she isn't Roxie.

"I am genuinely sorry we didn't work out. I didn't want to hurt you. I've tried to make it right. I haven't left you with nothing. I bought you a car, paid your security deposit plus six months of rent on your new place. You can start over, find a guy who—"

"Isn't in love with someone else?" She finished.

"Yeah," I said, letting her have her anger. "You deserve better than me."

That seemed to take a lot of the fight out of her. Maybe I made this harder than it had to be. Maybe instead of denying how I felt, instead of trying so hard to make it work with her… it would have been kinder of me to just walk away.

"Well, I won't argue with that." She crossed her arms over her chest.

I reached out and pulled her into a hug. She wasn't soft and curvy like Roxie; she didn't melt against me like she wanted to get closer. Not a single stirring of desire could be felt in my gut.

Tiffany surprised me by hugging me back. I half expected her to push me away, but then again, her anger was really just a front for the hurt I caused. Maybe she needed a hug… and the apology I just gave her.

When I pulled back, I grinned down at her ruefully. "So did you come here just to bust my balls?"

She gave me a little wicked smile. "You deserved it."

"Yeah. I did."

"And maybe," she said quietly, "I came to say good-bye."

"If you ever need anything, Tiff, you can come to me. I mean it."

She nodded. "Yeah, I know. You're not all bad, Adam."

"I hope you find everything you're looking for, Tiffany." I meant those words. I really wanted her to be happy.

"I hope you do to," she replied and tilted her head to the side. "Although, I think you already have."

I made sure she got to her car okay before I went back inside. I glanced up at the stage and remembered Roxie's final dance, the dance she did just for me.

Tiffany was right. I had found everything I was looking for.

Roxie was it for me.

13

Roxie

I dozed off and on all night, but every noise I heard had me jolting awake. When the sun finally started to rise, I fell asleep on the couch, still wrapped up in Adam's jacket.

A few hours later, I woke up feeling stiff and severely unrested. I hated getting up in the morning. It was my least favorite part of the day. I liked to sleep in late, hit the snooze button, and sleep longer. Morning was not my friend, but coffee was.

As I trudged bleary-eyed into the kitchen to put on a pot of coffee, my fuzzy brain reminded me that when I became a nurse, early mornings might be a must. I stood in the center of the kitchen, grouchy and brooding, while the coffee dripped into the pot. When there was enough for a cup, I snatched it out of the base and dumped it into a clean, white mug.

After adding a little vanilla creamer from the fridge, I cupped my hands around the cup like it was my savior and breathed in the sweet, strong aroma.

I felt sorry for people who didn't have coffee in their life.

It was tragic.

After a few hearty swallows, I sighed. Feeling slightly less disgruntled, I went and peeked out the blinds. No one was outside watching me. There was no red car. In fact, in the light of day with a comforting cup of coffee in my hand, I was left wondering if perhaps I had imagined it all.

I almost wished I had, but I knew better.

Craig wanted something. This wasn't the first time we'd broken up. We'd ended our relationship on several occasions. Sometimes it only lasted an hour. Sometimes a couple weeks. Once it lasted six months. Then I went back to him.

If only I'd been strong enough to not let him get to me. If only I'd realized then that loving someone didn't mean having to be with them. It was entirely possible to love someone from afar. And sometimes it was safer.

If I had stood my ground and not let him sweet talk me back into his life, then I wouldn't be having all these thoughts right now. I wouldn't be flinching every time the phone rang or waiting for him to show up in random places.

The truth was those six months we'd been broken up had been painful. I never felt free of him. I never felt relieved or like I was better off. I had missed him. I almost mourned our relationship and what could have been. He was my first love, my only love. The first few months we'd been together had been unlike anything I'd ever known.

He was my entire world.

When I wasn't with him, I counted the minutes until I was. He made me feel beautiful. He made me feel special and wanted. The chemistry between us was undeniable.

Until things started to change.

But even after that, it was hard to let go of what we had because there was this part of me that always thought it would come back. That if he loved me like that once, he would again.

I was naïve.

I was innocent.

And during those six months, I did everything I could to move on, to forget about the hurt he caused me, to forget about how much I loved him.

It wasn't easy, and then he started coming around again. He'd show up at my job. He'd leave presents on my windshield—things he knew I loved.

I was foolish because I thought he was the only thing that could take away the hurt. The hurt he inflicted. When he put his arms around me and I laid my head on his chest, that little bit of hope, that piece of my heart that he would always own, made me overlook the truth.

And so I went back to him.

Things were good.

For a couple weeks.

And then they were worse than ever.

But instead of spiraling down into a bleak hole, I realized something.

During those six months apart, something inside me had changed. Something hardened. I was no longer the innocent girl I was at seventeen. I was jaded. I was cynical.

Around that time, I met Harlow. She was my first friend in years. My only friend in years. One of the downfalls of being with Craig was when he became my entire world, there was no room in it for anyone else.

Yeah, I got out of the tiny town I grew up in. I thought I was moving to better, more exciting things and that Craig and I would be on an adventure.

I ended up with no friends, no family, and a guy who tried to control my every move. And the adventure I thought I was getting? It came in the form of a stripper pole.

Not in a million years did I ever think I'd be a stripper.

It was just another example of how my life had somehow changed—how I changed—and I'd not even realized.

But I met Harlow. She was hell-bent on being independent, on taking care of herself. I wanted to be that way. When I heard she needed a roommate, I knew it was my chance, maybe the last chance I had at getting out.

I knew Craig wouldn't let me go that easily, but after several months of living here and settling into my friendship with her and making plans for my life, I started to fall into a pattern of security. The night he showed up at the bar and Adam treated him to a punch-fest that led to him being hauled away in handcuffs, I thought he'd finally gotten the point.

I thought he'd leave me alone.

Then the phone calls started. The voicemail messages pleading for me to call him back. I ignored him. This time around, the pain wasn't as bad. The mere thought of him didn't make me ache. Like I said, I was harder, more jaded. I'd gotten back with him that last time, but there was a large part of myself I hadn't let him back into. It was almost as if, when we got back together, I realized it wasn't him I missed. It had been the memory of what we'd been all those years ago.

Maybe he sensed I wasn't coming back. Maybe he sensed he no longer had me under his thumb. It was making him desperate. Instead of calling, he was following me. The best thing I could do was ignore him. Pretend he wasn't even there. If he wanted to follow me, fine. I'd go about my life and let him see there was no place in it for him. He'd get bored. He'd move on. He'd shack up with one of his many "side items," and she would take over the position of being bullied by him.

I felt sorry for whoever she was.

I lifted the cup to take another sip of my coffee, but none flowed past my lips. I yanked the mug away and looked down. It was empty.

I shuffled back in the kitchen to get another cup and wandered into the bathroom and looked at myself in the mirror.

My reflection made me wince. I took another swallow of coffee, hoping it would fortify me for the sorry sight I made.

My eye makeup was rubbed around my eyes, making me look like a raccoon. My cheeks were pale and sunken, my lips looked chapped, my eyes were bloodshot, and my contacts felt entirely too dry.

I won't even tell you how bad my hair looked.

I wasn't an unattractive woman, but right now, I was downright hideous. After I pried the coffee from my hands and peeled off my clothes (carefully hanging Adam's jacket on the door), I got into a steamy hot shower.

I groaned out loud when the hot spray hit my back and tense muscles. After standing there for a long time just letting my body relax, I got to work with shampoo, deep conditioner, body scrub followed by moisturizing body wash, and a hydrating mask on my face. By the time I was done, the water was cool and the bathroom was filled with steam.

Once I was dry, I smoothed on my favorite coconut lotion and combed out my hair. Instead of covering up with my towel, I hung it up and pulled Adam's jacket around me and padded into my bedroom.

I laid the coat across my bed and looked at my fluffy pillows longingly. It was going to be a long day. After I dressed in cutoffs and a tank, I went back in the bathroom to blow-dry my hair and pull it into a high ponytail. I was too tired to do anything else with it.

I no longer had chapped lips (thank you ChapStick) or raccoon eyes, but they were still bloodshot and itchy. I took out my contacts and tossed them in the trash. After using a few eye drops and letting my eyes rest for a few moments, I put in a brand new pair. I just didn't feel like myself without them. My signature violet eyes were just so much better than my brown ones.

Since it was almost time to be at the club, I decided to stop on my way there to grab something to eat. Once I cleaned up the coffee and made sure the pot was off, I brushed my teeth and headed out.

It was hot, the air was thick and muggy, and the sky was overcast and gray. As I climbed in the car and started the engine, I couldn't help but anticipate seeing Adam today. I wondered if things would be different between us after that kiss. I wondered if he'd kiss me again.

I sat there with the car on for several minutes, waiting for the A/C to start cooling. As I sat there, I went through my phone to make sure I didn't have any missed calls or texts. I also got distracted by some video on the Internet about a kitten and a puppy.

Kittens and puppies make everything seem happier.

I backed out of my space and drove out to the main road. Sweat was gathering on the back of my neck, and it made me uncomfortable. "What the heck?" I said, glancing down at the A/C controls. It was on. I turned it on full blast and returned my eyes back to the road.

Something fluttering on my windshield caught my attention. I frowned and sat forward, trying to see what it was. It looked like a wrapper or something.

It had probably just gotten blown there last night in the rain.

As I was waiting for the traffic to clear so I could pull out on the main road, my eyes kept going back to the wrapper. Why wasn't it floating away? It was pinned beneath the windshield wiper.

Like it had been placed there.

I put the car in park and opened the door. I had to lift the wiper blade off it in order to pick it up. It was a piece of a SweeTarts wrapper. I frowned down at it as the traffic on the main road whizzed by. I flipped it over in my fingers, expecting to see the plain white wrapper on the back.

Call me.

The words were written in handwriting I knew all too well.

Another car pulled up behind me, and I hurried to get back in, shoving the note in my bag and getting back to driving. It was still hot as hades in here. I held my palm up to the vent. It was blowing hot air.

"Seriously!" I yelled. I just had this A/C fixed a couple months ago. They charged me out the ass for the repair. They said it needed a whole new pump or whatever.

I was pretty sure brand new air-conditioners worked longer than a couple months.

I rolled down my window and shut off the non-working I-got-ripped-off piece-of-crap A/C. Maybe instead of some food, I'd just get a smoothie. A cold one.

As I contemplated my flavor options, a red sports car pulled up behind me.

In the light of day, I didn't react like I had the night before. Or maybe I was just expecting it this time around.

I could see Craig sitting in the driver's seat, and while I really wanted to either:

A) Slam on my brakes and let the front end of his car get smashed

or

B) Stick my middle finger out the window and wave it at him furiously

Instead, I did what I promised myself I would do. I ignored him.

That didn't make him go away. By the time the smoothie place came into view, I was no longer hungry. I knew if I stopped, he would just pull over too. I didn't feel like dealing with it. I'd end up yelling at him for scaring me so badly last night. I was done yelling at him. It was a waste of breath.

He followed me all the way to the Mad Hatter.

My stomach churned when I signaled to pull in the lot, because I knew if he followed me, a conversation would be inevitable.

Surprisingly, when I turned, Craig kept driving. Thank you, God.

I parked right next to Adam's motorcycle near the entrance to the club. Just knowing he was inside and that I was going to be alone with him was enough to make me forget all about my stalker ex.

14

Adam

She might as well wear a label that read "handle with care." I'd never met a woman so prone to being an oxymoron as Roxie.

One minute she was strutting across the stage, almost naked and looking like a fierce sex kitten and then the next… the next she's pulling clothes around her and closing up the part of herself she doesn't want anyone to see.

But that part wasn't what my jacket covered.

It was a part deep down within her, buried beneath her skin and bones. For all of Roxie's sexy, independent, and quick-witted ways… there was another side to her. A side I often wondered if she even knew was there.

She was vulnerable. It was as if everything she let the world see was just armor to cover up the parts of herself she most needed to protect.

I told myself for years I didn't date her, didn't do anything about the heat she created in me, because she was my dancer. I told myself it was because she was taken. I told myself it was because I was taken.

As I lay awake last night, my dick refusing to soften, I realized something. Those things had only been excuses. I let those things keep me away from her.

Truth was she scared the shit out of me.

It only took one kiss for me to realize it.

That one kiss altered everything. I knew it would. I'd been dodging that kiss for almost two years. It didn't really make sense that I would run from something I wanted so badly.

Maybe Roxie wasn't the only oxymoron around.

It was that soft spot inside her that called to me the most. The intensity in which I wanted to protect her, to possess her, and to… *love* her made my body break out in a fine sheen of sweat.

How did a man not lose himself when someone like her was in his life?

She had the ability to consume me, to occupy my every waking thought. Hell, she already owned my cock. I'd already jacked off twice, yet it was still throbbing for her.

These last few months, things shifted between us. The desire I felt for her somehow grew, changed. It became more urgent. It was almost like something deep inside me was pushing me, telling me it was time for us.

I'd never admit it out loud, but I was still scared spitless. I wasn't sure it was the time for Roxie and me, but timing no longer mattered.

I kissed her.

I claimed her.

There was no going back.

Out in the club, I heard the heavy door open and bang shut. I moved automatically, pushing out of my desk chair and going to the open door. I knew it was probably Roxie, but I wasn't expecting her this early. She was padding across the hardwood in a pair of gray and neon-yellow sneakers in some sort of animal print. Atop her cutoff jean shorts sat a loose white tank halfway covering a neon-yellow top that sort of looked like a bra. What the fuck was she doing showing her bra off for everyone to see?

"Is that your bra?" I barked before I could think better of it. Women hated when men talked about their clothes, unless of course it was to tell them how awesome they looked.

Roxie stopped in her tracks and looked up. Her eyes widened and she seemed startled that I was standing here. Had she not seen me?

"What?" she said.

"I want to know why your bra is hanging out."

She gave me a look like I might have grown another head and then glanced down at herself, like she had no clue what she was even wearing. What the hell was wrong with her?

"It's a tank top…" she said, like it was obvious.

"That yellow thing is not a tank top," I growled.

She rolled her eyes. "It's a bandeau top. It's made to go under loose tops like this. It's stylish." As she talked, her dark ponytail bounced around on top of her head. Her dark bangs were pushed over to the side, revealing more of one purple eye than the other.

What the fuck was I doing talking about her clothes? "I don't like it."

"Too damn bad," she snapped. Then her shoulders slumped just enough for me to notice the movement. "You know what?" she said, straightening them. She huffed out a breath that ruffled her bangs, and she looked fucking sexy doing it. "I've had enough of men to last me a lifetime. Always trying to boss me around. I'm leaving."

She spun on her sneaker, the oversized white bag on her shoulder swinging around with her, and she marched toward the door.

I rushed after her. "Oh, no you don't," I growled, grabbing her elbow. She snatched herself out of my grip, but not before I felt her shaking.

"Hey," I said, gentling my tone. "What's wrong?"

"Nothing."

"It isn't nothing." Now that I wasn't staring at her hot body and way-too-revealing outfit, I focused on her face, on the way her mouth was drawn tight and the circles beneath her eyes. Added to the way I felt her trembling beneath my touch, I knew she was lying.

"I just don't feel that great," she said. "Can you train me tomorrow?"

My eyes narrowed as I considered ordering her to stay. And see, this is what I knew would happen. I was already rushing after her, trying to read her mood and gauging my words before I let them out of my mouth.

One kiss and I was already wrapped.

Fuck me.

She didn't wait for me to reply. She pulled open the door, ready to barge out into the sunlight. But she didn't. Instead, she froze. Her eyes seemed to focus on something outside, and then she slammed the door shut. "On second thought, let's just do it now."

"Woman, you're giving me whiplash," I rumbled. "What the hell is going on?"

"I don't want to talk about it," she said, avoiding my stare.

"Fair enough." I shrugged. If she didn't want to talk about it right now, fine. But she was going to tell me eventually.

"Really?" She seemed relieved, to the point that it made me feel bad.

"Yes, babe. Really." Remembering how she jerked away from me just seconds before, I made my movements deliberate, reaching for her hand and tangling our fingers together. She looked down at where we were joined and then back up at me.

I didn't know how to read the look on her face. It was a mix between fear, relief, and longing. She didn't pull her hand away.

"Come on," I said, leading her toward the office. "Let me show ya how to run this place."

15

Roxie

Two hours into my training and I had a whole new respect for Adam. He was good at what he did. Business was clearly something he excelled in. He was organized, thorough, and took a no-bullshit approach to everything concerning the club. It wasn't surprising at all he was very successful and opening a second place.

I also learned something about myself. Business bored the crap out of me. I understood what he was telling me, I understood the things I needed to do and keep an eye on, but the endless paperwork made me want to pour bleach in my eyes. It made me question my decision to take this new position.

Sharp snapping had me coming out of my boredom-induced coma, and I blinked, focusing on Adam, who was the one making the sound.

"Roxie, are you even paying attention?" Adam said, snapping his fingers together in front of my face.

"Of course." I lied.

"Yeah?" he said, amused, and set a stack of papers on his desk. "What did I just say?"

"Something about numbers," I answered evasively.

He chuckled. "You're bored out of your damn mind, aren't you?"

I sighed and plopped into a nearby chair. "Maybe this wasn't a good idea. Maybe I should go back to dancing."

"No." His response was swift and final.

"It's so boring," I whined. "How do you do this all day long?"

He grinned. "I like it."

"I'm going to be a terrible manager." I predicted.

"You couldn't be terrible if you tried," he rebutted. The affection in his rich tone made me smile a little. I loved the way he made me feel, as if I could sink right into him and curl up.

"I think that's enough for today," he said, walking over to where I was sitting.

"How much more is there to learn?" I groaned.

"Not too much."

Not too much = it was going to take forever.

"We can just finish, then," I said, wanting to get it over with.

"Or we could go grab something to eat."

I glanced up. "Eat?"

He nodded. "You look worn out, Rox. Have you eaten today?"

I planned on eating, until Craig decided to follow me around some more. "I had some coffee earlier."

"Let's go," he said, tossing the pen in his grasp down on the desk.

I hesitated, wondering if Craig was still sitting outside across the street from the club. Here I had been relieved when he kept driving, but he must've turned around and come back. It seemed odd he didn't sit in the parking lot instead of across the street.

"What's the matter," Adam said when I didn't get up. "Are you embarrassed to be seen with me?" I knew he was joking. The ornery grin on his face proved it.

But it wasn't funny.

His words struck a chord with me, reminding me of a time when someone (someone = Craig) was embarrassed to be seen with *me*.

Okay, so maybe he wasn't embarrassed so much as he didn't want all his flings to know he was involved with someone else. It took me a long time to figure that out. I was humiliated when I finally did.

One night I wanted to go see a movie, and I finally talked him into it. When we walked outside to leave, he wanted to take separate cars. To go to the same place.

I stood there dumfounded, asking him why on Earth we couldn't just drive together. He didn't answer. But he didn't have to.

The look on his face said it all.

It was the night I realized all the "rumors" about him cheating were true. Every whisper I heard when we went to the bar he liked or when his friends were over at our place was true. He'd always said people were just jealous, that his friends didn't like he wasn't always available to them because of me.

I should have known then it was a lie.

He was never available to me. Never.

Because he was out with other women. He had so many he didn't want to be seen driving around town with me.

We never made it to the movies that night. We got in a huge fight instead, and he left. Alone.

I didn't see him for two days.

"Roxie." Adam's soft voice broke me out of the memory, and I shook my head slightly to clear away the humiliation I still felt. Adam was kneeling right in front of my chair. His broad body filled the space in front of me and his thighs were spread so my knees were between them.

Because he was crouching low, he had to tilt up his head just slightly to meet my eyes. The deep-brown hue seemed to melt into me, the concern in his gaze flowing into me like hot lava, blanketing everything it touched.

"What's going on in that beautiful head of yours?" he asked, soft, reaching into my lap to entwine our fingers.

I glanced down at our joined hands, then back up at him.

"Kiss me."

He didn't need to be told twice. In seconds, he was standing to his full impressive height and towed me up along with him. Adam released my hand and cupped my face. His hands engulfed my jaw, but he was so gentle. His eyes swept over me like I was the most beautiful thing he'd ever seen, and around us, sparks flew like snowflakes in a blizzard.

Instead of crushing his mouth to mine like I expected, like I wanted, he took his time. His heated gaze dropped to my lips, then back to my eyes. His fingers spasmed against my head and tightened ever so slightly.

Slowly, slowly, he lowered his head, cupping my jaw so I could do nothing but hold still and wait for him to arrive.

The anticipation of his lips on mine was almost my undoing. Everything going on inside my head floated away. I became aware of the moment, of the quietness in the room, of the way my body swayed to get closer.

Adam's lips brushed over mine, a gentle caress, once, twice, and then a third time. He lifted his head just slightly and stared down at me. His thumb climbed up and caressed my lower lip.

He smiled softly and then joined our lips once more. This time he didn't lift his head. The kiss was soft and tender. It was a heavy kiss, the kind that settled within me like a weight, but it was the kind of weight that wasn't a burden.

When his tongue licked over my lips, I gladly parted for him, letting him inside my body, welcoming him.

No other parts of our bodies touched but our lips and his hands on my face. But I felt him everywhere.

This wasn't the kiss I had been expecting. I wanted hard and fast. Furious and passionate. I wanted something to chase away the terrible memories that crept up on me at unexpected moments and haunted me like unforgiving ghosts.

But Adam knew.

He knew exactly what it was I didn't know I needed.

A fast and furious kiss might have pushed the memories back into the shadows of my body, where they would lie and wait for the next opportunity to strike.

But this soft, tender… almost loving meeting of flesh made me unafraid of the memories. It took away their power. Yes, they might always be inside me, but shadows weren't so scary when one was filled with light.

"Adam," I whispered when he leaned his forehead against mine.

"Anything," was his whispered reply.

My stomach grumbled loudly, interrupting our perfect moment. His chest vibrated with laughter, and he stepped back. "C'mon."

He took my hand and led me through the club and outside. My eyes swept the area across the street as he locked up the door. I didn't see Craig, and the tension between my shoulder blades seemed to melt away.

"Wanna take the bike?" Adam asked, motioning toward his motorcycle.

"I've never been on a bike before," I admitted.

"So I'm your first?" I swear his ego and his head inflated about three sizes.

I rolled my eyes. "Yes, you're my first."

He grabbed a black helmet off the back and slid it down over my head. I thought my ponytail might get in the way, but instead, it made the helmet fit snugger so it didn't rattle around on my shoulders.

When it was buckled in place, Adam stood back to admire his handiwork. "You look like a bobble head." He grinned.

I tried to kick him, but he dodged my foot with ease, and I tipped over to the side. He caught me, setting me straight. "Careful there, sweetheart. You're top heavy now."

"Ass," I said, but my voice was completely muffled due to the massive protection around my skull.

He flashed his teeth, then straddled the bike. It was a Harley. Heat simmered in my core seeing him with all that metal and power between his legs.

Adam motioned for me, so I climbed on behind him. Reaching around, he looped my arms around his narrow waist and left his hand atop where my hands met. "Don't let go," he said.

I won't.

The bike rumbled and vibrated beneath us when he started it up and put it in motion. It was like being part of the wind. The way we navigated through the street seemingly without cause. Things looked different from the back of this bike. I felt free.

I didn't get to experience it very long, though, because he pulled into a Friday's just a mile down the street from the club. The parking lot was fairly empty because we'd arrived at a time past lunch but before dinner.

Once he slid the bike into an empty parking spot and supported it with its kickstand, shutting off the engine, I started to climb off. Adam grabbed my legs and stilled me, silently telling me not to move. I obeyed, wondering what he was doing as he spun around so he was straddling the bike, facing me.

The space between us was wide because our knees were bumping together, but that didn't last very long. Adam slid his palms in the hollow behind each knee and gave me a little tug. I slid forward, and he draped my legs over his thighs.

Our centers were intimately close. The only thing that kept me from rocking against him wantonly was the fact we were out in public.

Beneath my chin, Adam unbuckled the helmet and then tugged it off my head. I reached up to fix my undoubtedly helmet hair, but he caught my hand and pulled it against his lips. "Leave it," he murmured. "It's sexy."

The entrance to the restaurant opened, and a couple young guys came out. They were laughing, but when they saw us, they stopped. I knew from the flare in their eyes they noted the provocative way Adam and I were sitting.

I tensed a little, waiting for Adam to push me away or put some space between us.

He didn't.

The guys stepped off the curb, both of them openly looking at us, and walked to a nearby car. Adam glanced at them coolly, but they didn't seem to notice.

The blond-haired "surfer" type climbed in the passenger side, closest to us. Even after he got in the car, he turned to stare out his window. He gave me a little smile and jerked his chin at me through the glass.

Adam grasped me by the jaw and gently turned my face. His lips claimed mine in a thorough kiss. I forgot we were out in the open. I forgot we were being watched. Kissing him like this, practically in his lap where everyone could see, was such a high.

When he lifted his head, I licked my lips, loving the way he tasted. He grunted, satisfied, then looked at the car, which was now pulling away.

"What was that for?" I asked.

"Just letting everyone know you're already taken."

Surprise rippled through me. Not only was he unapologetically blatant about being here with me, but he basically just staked his claim.

How very caveman-ish.

Who knew cavemen were so sexy?

"I'm taken?" I asked, lifting an eyebrow.

He gave me a heart-stopping lopsided smile. "I'm working on it."

He was doing a damn good job.

Wait. *He was working on it?* Did that mean he wanted me?

Adam slid out from beneath me and tied the helmet to the back of the bike. When he was done, he pocketed the keys in his distressed jeans and allowed his eyes to roam over me for one lingering minute. When he was done, he made a half growl in the back of his throat and wrapped his hands around my waist.

"So tell me," he rumbled as he lifted me effortlessly off the bike. "How was your first time?"

His voice was sinful. Like some aged, insanely expensive bourbon that only rich people could afford. There was this lush flavor to his tone, like his words didn't come from his throat, but from the deepest parts of him. And when he lowered his usual tone, the effect was what I imagined finely aged bourbon would have. It was intoxicating.

"What?" I asked, breathless.

He laughed quietly as he slid my body down the front of his. It was a very effective way of showing me exactly how much he enjoyed our kiss.

"Your first time on a bike." He clarified, and it reminded me we were having a conversation.

"It was the best first time any girl could ever have."

"Words every guy wants to hear." He grinned.

"I've only ever said them to you."

I looked up at him from beneath my lashes, wondering if he understood that I was talking about more than just the bike ride. I knew he was only being playful and so was I, but I meant it. No one had ever given me a better first. It made me wish he'd been my first for more than a motorcycle ride.

"That's not your last first with me, sweetheart," he murmured and brushed a loose strand of hair away from my face.

I hoped not. I truly did. It scared me how much I wanted more firsts with Adam. I hadn't wanted anything or anyone so much since I met Craig all those years ago.

A little jolt of panic zinged around inside me with the thought. But then I felt my hand tucked inside Adam's, safe as he led me through the crowd toward the table the hostess escorted us to. And yeah, maybe I noticed the hostess note the way he caressed my lower back, gently motioning for me to slide into the booth before he moved to sit across from me.

Adam wasn't Craig.

I couldn't even define what was between us, but even still, he made me feel like I was the only woman in the room.

To any other girl, a guy acting like they were proud to have you on their arm was probably nothing new.

But for me…

Trashy

For me it was everything.

16

Adam

It was physically painful to sit across the table from her and resist the urge to touch her. I felt like I was back in high school all over again, just discovering the world of women.

And shit, I wanted to discover Roxie. I wanted to know every last detail about her, right down to the little sounds she made when I entered her.

Thoughts like that would only make it harder to sit here. I grabbed up my southern sweet iced tea and took a drink, telling myself to calm the fuck down. My hormones might be on overdrive, but sex wasn't the only thing I wanted from her.

Right now, I really wanted to know why the hell she looked so tired and where her mind would wander every so often. It was starting to worry me. I wanted to demand she tell me everything, but demanding anything from her would be a mistake.

Roxie didn't like pushy. She didn't like pressure; that much was obvious. I knew it was likely because that douche bag of an ex did a number on her.

If she didn't tell me, I was going to have to call Harlow. The circles under her eyes were unacceptable.

"You ready for tonight?" I asked, putting my tea back on the table.

She was swirling her straw around the soda she ordered. "I hope so," she replied.

"I'll be there tonight. I can introduce you around make sure everyone knows you're the boss."

She smiled. "How's the new club coming?"

"Good. Almost done. As soon as I have you trained, I'm going to start spending a lot of time over there."

Was that disappointment that flashed behind her eyes? I snatched her hand up off the table and rubbed my thumb across the back of her fingers. "Don't worry, Rox. I'll still have time for you."

She glanced up from the soda. "You mean in case I have any questions about work?"

I shook my head slowly. "I think you know what I mean."

The sound of a ringing phone interrupted whatever her response would have been. It was close and a little low, so I figured it had to be hers and it was in her bag.

She stiffened but otherwise made no move to answer.

I was glad because I wanted her all to myself.

The waitress came and delivered my sizzling tray of steak fajitas with all the fixins and a burger and fries for Roxie.

I liked a girl who ate. Most women ordered salad because they were always on a damn diet. I tried to tell 'em real men liked curves, but all the stick-thin models being broadcast all over TV made them think different.

It was a damn shame.

I watched in amusement as Roxie poured a huge amount of ketchup beside her fries, dunked one in, and took a bite. She made a little sigh of appreciation that had my loins tightening.

"You gonna have some fries with that ketchup?" I teased.

She popped the rest of the fry in her mouth. "You cannot eat fries without ketchup. Lots of it."

"If that's the way you like it, baby."

A change came over her, not really a visible one, but something shifted in the air. I looked up from the massive fajita I was assembling and saw her swallow thickly. "What is it?" I asked, automatically scanning the area around us for someone who appeared threatening.

"Don't call me that."

"Huh?" I asked, surprised I was the one who caused the change.

"Baby," she said, clearing her throat. "I don't like it."

She didn't like being called baby? What the fuck did that asshole do to her?

I tilted my head to the side. "How about sweetheart?"

She smiled, her shoulders relaxing. "I like that one."

"Sweetheart it is."

She went back to drowning her fries in ketchup, and I devoured my first fajita. Her phone started ringing again.

"Maybe you should get that," I said around a bite of steak.

She pulled her bag into her lap. It was so damn big it looked like a suitcase.

"What the hell do you need that giant sack for?" I asked.

She gave me a look that would wilt the weak. Good thing I wasn't weak. "It's not a sack, and it's for essentials."

"Essentials?" I echoed, wondering what the fuck she thought of as essential.

The phone continued to ring as she searched around the endless bag of "essentials," looking for it. The tone cut off and she paused in searching.

Then it started ringing again.

"Maybe it's an emergency," I said.

Roxie pulled out a handful of crap and laid it on the table and continued to search out her phone. When she found it, she said, "Ah-ha!" like it was some sort of major victory.

I thought it was cute as hell.

Her face paled slightly when she looked at the screen. Then she hit a button, silenced the ring, and dropped it back into the sack. "I don't recognize the number," she said.

She was lying.

A bad feeling wormed its way into my gut.

"Roxie," I intoned.

She pretended she was busy scooping up the items on the table to put back. As she did, a torn piece of paper fluttered toward my plate.

It was a note that read, *Call me.*

Two words never incited so much jealousy.

I snatched it up before she could. I had no idea who it was from, but instantly, I didn't like them. "You have an admirer?"

"No," she said, reaching for the paper.

That bad feeling reared up again, and I knew. "Is he bothering you again?"

"Adam…"

"Is he the reason you don't want me to call you baby?" I pressed.

"Does it matter?" she whispered.

"I think it does," I replied.

The scrap of paper fell between us on our table. It might as well have been the Grand Canyon. Just like that, she pulled away. So far away she was nearly unreachable.

"You know you're safe with me, right?" I said, leaning across the table.

Roxie snatched up the paper and crumpled it into a ball before dropping it back in her sack.

"And I don't mean that in a totally romantic comedy type of way."

That earned me a smile.

"You are safe with me that way too," I added. "I'm not gonna hurt you." I knew she was listening even though she kept her eyes away from mine. So I continued. "I'm talking about the kind of safety where you can tell me anything. The kind of safety where nothing you say will ever change the way I see you."

"How do you see me, Adam?" she asked. Damn if that vulnerable piece of her wasn't visible in her eyes.

"I see you as completely lovable, every last part of you."

"I have scars you can't see." I noted the small catch in her voice.

"We all do, sweetheart," I said, laying my hand palm up on the table between us. I wiggled my fingers, inviting her.

She wavered.

"Your scars are beautiful, Rox, just like the rest of you. Your scars mean you were stronger than whatever—*whoever*—tried to hurt you."

She slid her hand into mine.

Victory.

I gave it a gentle squeeze before pulling back. "Eat your ketchup," I ordered and snagged a strip of steak off my plate and dunked it in her red stuff before shoving it in my mouth.

I winced. "That's basically a crime against good meat," I said as I chewed.

She laughed and started to eat.

"So how did you end up a business man?" she asked.

I rolled with the topic change because I knew trying to talk about the note and her ex wouldn't go so well. Besides, it was a conversation we needed to have in private.

"You mean how the hell did I end up owning a strip club?" I rephrased the question.

"Yeah." Roxie grinned.

"It sort of just happened." I shrugged, thinking about where my life was supposed to go.

She tilted her head and waited for me to continue. I worked on making up the rest of my fajitas as I talked.

"I used to play football."

"Like in high school?" she asked.

I nodded. "I started in sixth grade. Played all through high school. It was my entire life."

I still remembered the rush I got every time I ran out onto the field, the crowd was roaring from the stands.

"Were you any good?"

"Was I any good?" I scoffed. "I was the fucking bomb."

"Were you now?" she asked, amused.

"I wanted to go pro, be in the NFL."

"I had no idea," she said, picking up her soda to sip at it.

I shrugged. "I don't talk about it much."

"So what happened?"

"I got a full ride to LSU. Got tapped by them before I even graduated high school. The plan was to go to college, make a name for myself on the field, and get drafted before I even completed my degree."

"You went to LSU?" she asked.

"For almost two years," I said, abandoning my plate and thinking back to the moment that changed my life forever. Most people can't pinpoint the exact time nothing would ever be the same again. But I could. "I got injured, tore my ACL, had to have some surgeries. My dream of the NFL went down the drain the second I heard that tendon snap."

"Adam," Roxie said, her voice full of empathy.

"I lost my scholarship. My first wife… It was a dark period in my life," I said, not wanting to relive those first few weeks when I realized I wouldn't be playing football again.

"You were married in college?" she asked.

I nodded. "Married my high school sweetheart. I was the quarterback; she was the head cheerleader.

She came to LSU with me and we got married. Turns out she didn't really love me. She only loved the future NFL pro. When she realized that wasn't going to be in my future, she decided she wasn't going to be either."

"What a bitch," Roxie said.

I grinned. "So I left college, took a bunch of business classes, and moved here. I bought the Mad Hatter not too long after, and here I am."

"It must have been a lot of work to make the club as successful as it is today," Roxie said, giving me a smile.

I shoved the rest of the last fajita into my mouth and regarded her as I chewed. After I swallowed, I said, "I don't shy away from hard work. If I want something, I won't stop until it's mine."

And I want you.

By the fine blush that spread across her cheeks, I knew she caught my double meaning.

At least she couldn't say I didn't warn her.

17

Roxie

He wouldn't stop calling.

He was getting more persistent. I knew by the way Adam looked at me he was suspicious.

Why wouldn't Craig just go away? He made me feel claustrophobic, like I couldn't breathe, like I could barely move.

All I wanted was for him to let me go so I could fully move on. It seemed like every time I took two steps forward, he'd pull me back one. I felt like a hamster on a wheel, running and running but never getting anywhere.

I was tired.

It was hard to sit across from Adam and fully enjoy spending time with him, because my inner thoughts kept thinking about my past and how it was bleeding into my present and threatening my future.

After we finished lunch, we parted ways, Adam going home to change out of his jeans and T-shirt and me coming home to change as well. Harlow still wasn't home when I got here. She must have been getting ready for work at Cam's today.

Being in this empty apartment was slightly unnerving. All I could think about was last night and how Craig followed me.

Don't let him take away your home. I willed myself.

I would not let Craig make me scared to be here.

I had a little time before I needed to be back at the club, so I plugged in a large-barrel curling iron to let it heat while I got dressed. For my first night as acting manager of the Mad Hatter, I put on a fitted black skirt that was short enough to look sexy, but not short enough to be unprofessional. Maybe this skirt wouldn't have been appropriate if I worked at a bank, but I didn't. I worked at a strip club, and even as manager, I wanted to look good.

Over the skirt, I added a fitted white tank top and a black lace T-shirt. I put on my black heels and then went in the bathroom to apply some makeup and attack my hair. Getting my dark, straight strands to hold a curl was challenging, sometimes impossible. Harlow taught me a trick though to help, and I pulled out a can of setting spray. As I sectioned off lengths of hair, I spritzed it with the spray and then wound my hair around the heated barrel. After holding it in place for long seconds, I slid it out to reveal and perfect spiral. I sprayed it with even more spray and then let it cool as I went to work repeating the process over and over until all my strands were curled.

When I was done and all the curls were cooled and the hairspray was dry, I flipped my head upside down and loosened the coils with my fingertips. Amazingly, I achieved the effect I was going for. Large, loose, shiny curls fell over my shoulders and back. I really hoped the style held tonight.

I wanted to look pretty. For Adam.

After giving my hair yet another squirt of hairspray, I added some deep-pink lipstick, smiling a little remembering how Adam had looked with it smeared on his mouth.

Before heading for the door, I grabbed a cropped, lightweight red jacket that looked like leather but wasn't and slid it on. My hair took longer than I thought it would, so I rushed toward the door, not wanting to be late.

I flung open the door to rush outside but stopped short when I nearly collided with something standing in the doorway of the apartment.

I gasped loudly as my heart leapt into my throat. My hand gripped the wooden doorframe to keep myself from tumbling over with the force of my halt.

It was Craig.

He looked at me through dark lashes. "Hey, baby."

My stomach tightened and this sick feeling came over me. I did not want to see him right now.

"What are you doing here?" I demanded. "And what the hell have you been following me around for?"

He acted like he didn't notice my bitchy tone. But I knew it was an act. "Can I come in?"

"No."

The corners of his eyes tightened. "I just wanna talk, Roxie. I came by last night. I asked you to call me."

I snorted. "You didn't come by," I snapped. "You were creeping around like some weirdo."

He sighed and pushed past me into the apartment. I thought about taking off my shoe and giving him a good whack with the heel. I didn't want him here. "Please go." I didn't shut the door. I left it open and kept myself rooted right beside it.

Craig turned. His hands were casually draped in his jeans and he rolled his hips forward as he walked closer. Damn him for looking so good. Damn me for noticing.

"I miss you, baby," he said, his voice low as he stopped just in front of me. "You look real good."

It wasn't going to work. Not this time. I wasn't going to fall for this. He might be my first love, the keeper of a lot of my firsts, but he wasn't going to be my only.

"It's over, Craig. We aren't getting back together. Stop calling me. Stop following me. You aren't welcome here."

"Roxie." The way he spoke my name was almost like an admonishment, like we both knew that what I just told him was a lie. Like we both knew when he turned up the charm, I'd come rushing back into our old patterns.

I lifted my chin and stared at him. I looked him straight in the eyes, not wavering at all. I wanted him to see it. I wanted him to know this time was different.

He must have seen what I intended.

Unfortunately, it pissed him off.

His baby blues went flat and hard. At his sides, his hands fisted. "It's him, isn't it?" he intoned.

"What?" I asked, standing my ground even though I wanted to take a step back.

"Are you fucking him?" Craig growled, angry. He was a possessive guy, and it wasn't really in a protective sort of way. It was a selfish, controlling kind of possession he harbored.

"No," I said, recoiling. I knew he was talking about Adam. Adam was the only other man I'd ever really looked at since high school.

"Don't you fucking lie to me!" he snapped and shoved me against the door. Because it was open, the force of my body pushed it back and it banged against the wall.

"I'm not!" I insisted. He was pinning me against the wood, his hand on my throat. I felt his fingers wrapped around me and I knew I was only one hard squeeze away from not being able to breathe.

My body wanted to tense up. My heart was beating so hard it hurt. Panic pushed through my blood vessels, wanting to take over my entire body.

But I couldn't let it.

Showing him I was scared only made it worse.

If he was going to hit me, if he was going to threaten me this way, then I would act like I didn't care. I wouldn't bow down to him. Not ever.

"I saw you," he growled, shoving his face right up to mine. The putrid scent of lingering liquor on his breath made my stomach churn. God, I hated that smell.

It was the scent of anger, abuse. If Craig had been drinking before he came here, then this wasn't going to end well. It wouldn't matter what I said. Talking him down was almost impossible when he was drunk.

I never knew alcohol could make a person mean. Even though I worked in a bar, I was now severely uncomfortable with drunk men. They were unpredictable. It brought out the truth in them… It brought out their dark sides.

It was always something I could keep hidden, the way my body reacted around a drunk man. At the club, it was always under control. Adam wouldn't put up with any kind of disrespect, and everyone knew it and the bouncers enforced it.

But I wasn't at the Mad Hatter. There was no bouncer to make sure Craig behaved.

"What the hell were you at the club so early for today?" he accused. "All alone in that building with him. With the boss. How long have you been doing him?"

I shook my head.

He pulled me away from the door and then slammed me back into it. My shoulders took the brunt of the hit and my back stung.

"I'm not sleeping with Adam!" I insisted. "He's my boss. He gave me a promotion."

It was the wrong thing to say.

"A promotion, huh? You're a little slut. Blowing the boss for more cash. You're nothing but trash."

Anger lit through me. How dare he talk to me like this! "Get your hands off me," I growled, looking right into his eyes.

His hand tightened around my throat, threatening to crush my windpipe. "Come on, fucker," I taunted. "Do it."

His eyes flared. Instead of doing what I challenged, he yanked me away from the door again. My feet skidded across the floor as I tried to gain some traction. His hand left my throat and he gripped me by the shoulders. His fingers cut into my arms even through my clothes, and I winced.

"You're mine. We aren't done. No one else is allowed to touch you," he hollered. He began to shake me, like he could somehow talk some sense into me.

"Stop it." I gasped as my head rolled on my shoulders with the force of his shoves.

"I swear to God, if I see you with him again, I will fucking kill him."

Fear like none other slammed in to me. The thought of him hurting Adam made me physically sick, and I gagged. How dare he threaten Adam! It was sad, but I'd grown accustomed to his threats against me, but threatening someone else because of me… this was new.

He continued to shake me. My teeth rattled. I reached out to steady myself, taking fistfuls of his T-shirt. "Stop," I stuttered, grasping him.

Craig gave me one last shove, and I heard a snap. I stumbled back when he let go of me, and I glanced down at my hand. The gold chain he always wore around his neck was dangling from my palm. It had been caught in the shirt when I grabbed it and his shove made the chain break.

Horror filled me. *Oh no.*

I looked up at Craig. His eyes were wide and angry. His nostrils flared as he looked at his broken possession. Then he tore his gaze away from it and pinned me with a hot stare.

"It was an accident," I swore. "You shoved me."

Craig gave an angry shout and snatched the chain out of my palm. "You're going to pay for this." He snarled and grabbed me by the front of my shirt.

"I can get it fixed," I vowed, hating the way I rushed to make it right. This was his fault, but my bravado was gone. I was scared now. He was pissed.

He dragged me across the room and threw me on the couch. My back hit the front and bowed around it. Pain exploded, but I didn't have time to think about it because he picked me up and tossed me onto the cushions and straddled my hips. The slap he delivered across my face stung and made my eyes water. I turned my head, letting my hair cover my face and eye as I stared at the plain-colored couch cushions as the ache radiated across my cheekbone.

"You think you can go out with him and me not know!" he roared. "You think you can straddle the back of his bike and press yourself against him and me not know! You're trying to make a fool out of me!" he snapped. "I won't have it."

He grabbed my chin, squeezing and forcing my head around so I had to stare up into his angry face.

How can someone so good-looking be so ugly?

I didn't say anything even though I wanted to yell. There was a difference between bravery and stupidity. He was sitting on me, pinning me down. Whatever I said right now would only make it worse.

"Do you understand me?" he said, chest heaving.

I nodded as his fingers dug into my jaw.

He got up abruptly. His weight leaving me was such a relief. I scrambled up to my feet, pushing my hair out of my face and glaring at him.

He threw the chain at me. It hit me in the stomach and fell at my feet. "I want that fixed. Today."

"I want you out of my life." My voice was deadly calm, utterly serious. I couldn't do this anymore. I wouldn't.

His eyes narrowed. He stalked toward me. My body prepared itself for another blow. "You want him that bad?"

"This has nothing to do with Adam," I ground out.

"Don't you fucking say his name to me!" he roared. I winced and my ears rang. Surely, the neighbors could hear him… Why wasn't anyone helping?

"You make me sick," he said, his voice quieter. "I thought you were better than that."

I didn't know what he was talking about. How could he imply that any attraction I might feel toward Adam was wrong? Adam was ten times the man he would ever be.

He heaved a heavy sigh. "I'll let you go."

My eyes snapped up to his. I wanted so desperately to believe what I just heard.

He chuckled. "The desperation in your eyes is not a good look," he spat.

"What do you want?" I asked. I didn't care if I sounded desperate. I was.

"I need you to do something for me," he said, his voice finally back in control. "Do it and you won't have to see me again."

I clung to this sudden ribbon of hope, even though I knew it was probably a lie.

He reached into the back pocket of his jeans and withdrew a business card and extended it to me. I took it but didn't look away from him. I wanted to be aware of what he was doing at all times.

"In two days, be at that address. The time is on there. Come dressed like the trash you are and be ready to perform."

Perform?

A sinking, sick feeling settled in my gut. *Oh no…*

I glanced down at the card. **PINK PRODUCTIONS.**

I snapped my head up. "I told you no," I growled.

He shuffled closer and grabbed my chin again. My jaw already hurt from how he grabbed it earlier. I struggled to pull away. His hands made me sick. How the hell I ever got pleasure out of them I would never ever understand.

He tightened his grip and stepped even closer so I could feel the muscles beneath his clothes. I wanted to sag in defeat. His sheer size and muscle mass outmatched me tenfold.

"I told you it was a done deal," he said quietly. "I've already been paid. The money's been spent."

So that's how he paid for that car…

"You *will* do this, Roxie," he intoned. "And in return, I'll get out of your life."

I felt tears well in my eyes. Damn him! Damn my weaknesses, damn my anger, and damn my fear.

His eyes softened. "Don't cry, baby," he crooned. "I love you."

Oh my God, was that supposed to make me feel better?

Finally, he released my chin and stroked the side of my head, like he was petting a dog or a possession. "Just do this for me."

I'd rather die.

"You wouldn't want anything happen to lover boy, would you?"

That got my attention. I might give up my life, but not Adam's.

He smirked. "I thought so." Craig stroked my hair again. "Be at that address day after tomorrow, Roxie. Come dressed like the trashy bitch you are."

He stepped away, but I felt no relief.

Causally, he strolled toward the door like he didn't have a care in the world, like hitting and threatening someone he supposedly *loved* was natural.

He turned in the open doorway before leaving and gave me the kind of charming smile I fell for when I didn't know any better.

"And, Roxie? Wear your hair like that. It looks hot."

When he was gone, I sank down onto the sofa, my entire body trembling. I sat there for a long time, numb and staring off into space. Reality eventually came creeping back, and I felt the heavy card crushed in my hand.

I looked down and a sob ripped from my throat.

I was finally getting what I wanted. I was getting rid of Craig.

The price for my future was very steep.

PINK PRODUCTIONS.

It sounded innocent, almost pretty.

It was none of those things.

Craig tried to sell me to them before, and I wouldn't have it. Seems he somehow made a deal behind my back. He pretty much sold me to a company with no morals at all.

The price for my freedom and apparently Adam's safety…

Trashy

Starring in a porn flick.

18

Adam

She was late.

Roxie was never late.

She was probably just nervous, fussing over her hair or some shit, and lost track of time. But the more I told myself that, the harder it got to believe.

Harlow poked her head in my office as I looked at the clock. "Has Roxie called in?" she asked.

I muttered a profanity. "No. She hasn't called you?"

She shook her head, worry in her eyes.

"Did you see her before work?" I asked.

A guilty expression crossed her face. "I knew I should have stayed home," she said almost to herself.

I motioned for her to come into the office. "What the hell does that mean?" I asked as she walked in.

"I haven't seen her. I stayed at Cam's last night."

That bad feeling in my gut intensified. "Is there a reason you look guilty?"

Harlow sighed and averted her eyes.

"Spill it," I ordered.

"I think he's bothering her again," she admitted.

I knew she was going to say that. I mean, I'd pretty much been thinking the same thing, but just hearing the words out loud pissed me off. "What makes you think that?"

"He's been calling. Blowing up her phone," Harlow said. "I asked her about it. She doesn't say much, but…"

"What?"

"She's been a little jumpy lately."

"Fuck."

"She was home alone last night." Harlow worried, wringing her hands. "I offered to stay home, but she told me to go."

That would explain the dark circles beneath her eyes and her distracted head.

"It's my fault—"

I held up my hand. "No, it isn't. Roxie is stubborn as hell."

"Still, I think I might be all she has." She said it softly, like it hurt to voice aloud.

It fucking hurt to hear.

"She has me," I ground out.

Harlow glanced up, her eyes wide. "I thought you two were just friends."

I gave her a level stare. "You know better."

She smiled. "Yeah, I do. Glad you finally do too."

I grunted and reached into my pocket and pulled out my keys. "Can you keep an eye on the place? I'm going to check on her."

Harlow nodded.

I shut my office door on the way out and scanned the crowd already forming in the bar. Cam was behind the bar, and I knew he and Harlow would be able to handle things here.

I nodded at Ty, the best bouncer in the place, on the way out and stepped into the parking lot. It was still light out, but because it was late summer, it wasn't as bright as it would have been just last month.

I turned the corner of the building toward my bike and collided with Roxie.

She bounced off my chest and I reached out to steady her. I couldn't help but notice all the dark curls falling over my fingers.

"Roxie," I said. Relief flooded my system. "I was just coming to check on you."

"I'm sorry I'm late," she said. Her voice was slightly off. Forced. "I lost track of time."

She was shaking again. I felt the slight trembling beneath my hands.

"Hey," I said, releasing her. "You okay?"

She glanced up at me, then ducked her head. Her face was red. I went to grasp her chin to look at her again, but she flinched.

Rage burned through me. It ate away all the worry I had for her just moments ago. I'd never had a woman flinch away like she was scared.

"Look at me, Rox."

She did, letting her curls fall around her face. Her cheeks were flushed, her skin uncomfortably red. "Why is your face so red?" I asked.

"Oh," she sighed. "The A/C in my car went out. I'm just hot."

"Didn't you just have that fixed?" I asked suspiciously. I was suddenly taken back to the night I sent her home because of that damn non-working

A/C. She was sick from the heat, and I told her to go. I'd ultimately sent her home to be attacked.

It was the night I slept on her couch.

"Apparently, the guys at the garage thought they could charge me full price and slap a Band-aid on it to make me think it was working again."

I clenched my jaws. What kind of asshole takes money for a job, then lets a woman drive off in the heat, knowing the problem wasn't fixed?

I muttered exactly what kind of asshole I thought he was. Roxie laughed, her head tipping back with the force of her giggle.

She had a handprint around her throat.

My vision dimmed and went dark around the edges. Her cheeks might be red from the lack of A/C, but the redness around her jaw and the markings on her throat were not because she was hot.

"Sweetheart." My voice was heavy. I didn't know how to feel such strong emotions simultaneously.

Rage and regret threatened to choke me.

Her eyes flashed, and I knew she realized what I'd seen. Quickly, she ducked her head and let her hair fall around her neck and over her shoulders.

Even so, what I'd seen could not be unseen.

"We're leaving," I said, motioning for her to move toward my bike.

"I'm here to work."

"We need to talk."

"No, we don't," she said. I saw the panic sweep into her eyes.

"What are you so afraid of?" I whispered. *Why won't you talk to me?*

Her shoulders slumped. The stubbornness she always carried wasn't there. "Right now?" she whispered. "Everything."

I wanted to grab her and yank her to me. I was afraid to. I was afraid she would flinch away or that I would scare her.

Fuck. That.

I wasn't going to let that fuckwad influence the way I treated Roxie. I wouldn't give him any power over me at all. He already had too much. If Roxie didn't want me to hold her, she could tell me herself.

I reached for her, gently tugging her wrist. "Come here."

She melted against me. It wasn't the first time I'd had Roxie in my arms, but she felt smaller than ever. I had to stomp down on the rage inside me because she didn't need that kind of emotion. She needed something else, something better.

Something I was pretty sure not many people had given her before.

I tucked her against me, fitting her head just beneath my chin. The way she curled into my chest, like she couldn't get close enough, made my heart trip. Roxie pulled her arms so they were under her, against my chest, and gripped the front of my dress shirt.

I rubbed up and down her back and didn't say a thing. I just held her close, feeling like a fish out of water. I didn't know how to act in a situation like this. I'd never had any experience with a man who fucking beat a woman.

I wanted to kill him.

Honest to God. If he were standing here right now, I would've fucking killed him.

Men—*no*—people in general who took advantage of someone smaller, someone more vulnerable, were scum.

But how could I do that without hurting her worse?

A couple people on their way into the bar gave us sideways stares as they walked past. I gave 'em the eye, daring them to say a word. They didn't, having gotten the message.

"Sweetheart," I murmured, tightening my hold. "Let's go talk."

She made a sound like she didn't want to move, like it was early morning and someone was trying to get her out of bed.

I smiled. Guess that meant she thought I was comfortable.

"We can't stand outside all night," I said, amused and feeling pretty damn smug.

She stiffened and then snatched herself away from me in two seconds flat. The way her eyes darted around with fear and the way the blood leeched from her skin had my jaws clenching again.

Was she afraid someone might see us?

That *he* might see us?

I took her hand, ignoring the way it stayed stiff and towed her toward the entrance to the club. Ty opened the door and seemed a little surprised to see us both there.

I put Roxie right beside him. "Watch her, Ty," I ordered.

I didn't bother to see if this pissed her off, because frankly, I didn't care. I stalked into the bar and pinned Cam with a stare. Harlow was standing nearby, giving him an order of drinks. Both of them looked up.

"Cam, you're in charge."

Cam just nodded. Harlow's eyes got wide.

"You help him," I told her.

"Roxie?" She started forward.

I held up my hand. "I got this."

She started to protest, but Cam called her name and her steps faltered.

"I'll handle things here," Cam said.

I trusted him. I knew the Mad Hatter would be fine tonight. For once in my life, I really didn't care. I wasn't worried about my business; I was worried about Roxie.

It was a little startling to realize I'd never put any of my four wives above this place. Maybe that's why I was divorced.

Nah. They were just bitches.

Roxie was still right next to Ty when I walked out. "Thanks, Ty."

"See ya later, boss!" he called after us as I led Roxie toward my bike.

"My bike or your car?" I asked.

"Oh, I have a choice?" she snapped.

I pinned her with a stare. "I told you, you always have a choice with me."

Her lower lip wobbled.

I groaned. "Rox, you wanna come with me?"

I wanted this to clearly be her choice.

She nodded.

I straddled my bike and reached for her. She started to climb on behind me, but I made a noise and stopped her. "Uh-uh. Up here."

I patted the seat in front of me and scooted back to make a spot for her between my thighs.

"I can't drive that thing," she said.

"I'll drive."

"You can drive with me sitting there?"

I gave her a look. She sighed and climbed on, fitting between my thighs perfectly. Once she was settled, I scooted closer so my chest was pressed along her back. Our legs were forced together, and I reached around her to grab the handlebars.

I didn't want her behind me. I didn't want her to feel exposed or somehow vulnerable. This way she could feel more protected and I could feel her in my arms.

"You ready?" I asked low right beside her ear.

She nodded and curled her hands around my knees.

The bike roared to life beneath us, and I steered it away from the Mad Hatter and in the direction of my place.

It was the first time I'd ever driven a bike with someone practically in my lap. The feel of her relaxing against me and the sensation of her silky curls flying out and wrapping around my arms made me want to do it more often. With her. Only with her.

I lived in a condo on the beach. It cost too much money, but I didn't care. I liked getting up and running right on the sand. I liked the view from the window, and I liked the gated security that came with the building. After I opened the Mad Hatter II and got it rolling, my next business purchase was going to be a complex like this. The guy who owned this place had to be making bank for what he charged for rent. I wanted in on the action.

The guard was surprised when I pulled up with Roxie on the front of my bike. To his credit, he didn't say anything, just pressed the button and waved me through. I saw Roxie glancing at the gate as we drove past it, and I hoped it made her feel safe and not trapped.

The spot right beside my car, a two-seater BMW, was open, so I parked and cut the engine. Roxie didn't move. I could feel her hesitation.

"You know I just wanna talk," I said.

"That's what I'm afraid of."

"Please don't be afraid of me." I breathed the words into her ear.

She shivered lightly, and I wrapped an arm around her waist.

"It isn't you I'm afraid of," she said. "It's the way you're going to look at me when I tell you what you want to know."

I reached up and slid all the hair over the back of her shoulder, tucking it out of the way and revealing the side of her cheek. I nuzzled the soft skin on her face, pressing lingering kisses to her cheekbone.

"Give me a little more credit than that, sweetheart."

She turned her face into my kiss. I wrapped my other arm around her, and she tilted her face upward so I could reach her lips.

I kissed her slow and light. The way our lips brushed together like two feathers floating from the sky had my loins tightening. I pulled back slightly and kissed the corner of her mouth, letting my tongue dart out to tease the fullness of her lips, and she sighed.

I forced myself off the bike and led the way up the stairs to my condo.

As we walked, I steeled myself for what she was about to say, because I knew whatever it was, I wasn't going to like it.

19

Roxie

The view out his windows beckoned me. He had an almost panoramic view of the ocean. The sun was sinking and appeared as a great orange ball floating across the edge of the water. The sky was streaked with peach hues, and the white moving caps of the surf seemed to float on forever.

The sand was inviting, making my toes squirm in my heels, wanting to get out to play, to sink down into the gritty sun-warmed grains.

I couldn't imagine waking up to this every day. I'd never want to leave.

"Like it?" Adam asked, coming up beside me to stare out across the view.

"It's gorgeous," I said, but even the breathtaking views couldn't keep my eyes from looking at him.

"I run down there every single morning," he rasped, his voice rough like the crashing waves.

"I'm going to have to start running too, since I'm not going to be dancing every night."

"You're perfect the way you are, Rox," Adam said, turning his head and looking at me.

We got lost in the moment, the two of us. We stood there in the sinking sunlight of early evening staring at each other, studying every last nuance of each other's face. It was quiet here, but a comfortable sort of quiet. The kind that sometimes seemed elusive.

The moment broke when Adam's eyes darkened and he brushed his knuckles over my jaw and trailed them down to my neck. The flesh was still sore. I prayed it didn't leave marks, but I was terribly afraid they were already starting to form. In fact, I knew they were, because Adam's eyes tightened when he looked in that direction.

"I don't play games," Adam said as he drew his hand back. "I don't like them."

I looked back out at the ocean as he spoke.

"You and I have been dancing around each other for years, Rox. I think we both knew this was inevitable."

"What?" I turned my head to stare at him once more.

"That you and I… we're going to happen."

Yeah, I did know. For a long time, I thought Adam was only a fantasy, someone who would slip through my fingers, but I was wrong.

"I want you, Roxie," he said clear as day. "I've wanted you a long time. It never felt like the right time," he said, and I nodded because he was right. "I'm tired of waiting for the right time. Tell me you want me."

"I want you," I echoed. I wanted him so badly that sometimes it hurt.

Adam reached for me, but I evaded him, pacing across the dark wood floors. "But I'm not good for you," I said. "I've got a lot of baggage, Adam, and I'm very afraid some of it may never go away."

"I've got plenty of baggage of my own," he said with a sardonic grin.

Yes, but even his four ex-wives combined couldn't match the shit storm that was Craig.

"You don't understand," I told him, sorrow creeping into my tone. "Being with me isn't safe for you."

"I think I can handle ya," he said, amused.

But it wasn't funny. Nothing about this was. My chest ached so badly I thought it might split in two. How had my life come to this?

"Roxie?" Adam said, finally realizing I was being all too real.

I turned back to him. He'd come closer. He was right beside me, staring into me with his chocolate eyes.

"He threatened you, Adam." My voice cracked. "He saw us together. He's so angry and…" My voice cracked again and I drew in a shaky breath.

He draped his arm across my shoulders and steered me to a giant, sleek-looking sofa in the center of the room. It was grounded by a gray-and-white striped carpet and glass coffee table.

"Why don't you start from the beginning?" Adam said, pulling me down beside him.

I faltered. Did I really want to show him all my skeletons? Did I really want him to know just how pathetic I really was?

"I'm not going anywhere," he said. "The more you tell me, the more I can help."

Help.

I never thought I needed help before. I was used to being on my own, dealing with this alone. Maybe that's why everything seemed so damn hard. Maybe I needed help. Maybe I needed Adam.

"I met Craig when I was seventeen." I began. "I grew up in a town I only wanted to leave. Getting out was my only plan."

He nodded, encouraging me to go on.

"And then I met Craig."

I felt the change come over him, but he held it back so I wouldn't stop. I paused because I felt like just barging in with the story about Craig didn't really tell the full story. Because really, this was about me. For Adam to understand how I ended up in this position, he needed to know *me.*

"When I was in high school, I wasn't datable," I told him.

He gave me a look that would make lemons rot, and I smiled. I loved that he rejected that idea so readily. It's like he could never think of me as anything but datable.

I smiled and turned, settling my side against the back of the couch and facing Adam. "I really wasn't. No one ever asked me out. I was the friend, the buddy, the cute one. I never went to a school dance because no one ever asked me, and I was too insecure to go by myself. I thought it would make me look pathetic."

"What the hell was wrong with the boys in that town? Were they blind?" Adam asked.

I laughed. "To me? Yes. At least when my best friend was standing there. She was blond and beautiful, the kind of girl that drew all the eyes in a room."

"I wouldn't have noticed her," he said softly. "I would have been too busy looking at you."

I leaned my head against the cushion and smiled. "Anyway, I told myself I didn't want a boyfriend anyway, that I wanted out of the town more. I never partied. I never drank or smoked. I got really good grades, and I had a good reputation."

"Ahh, a good girl." He smirked.

I poked him in the ribs. "See, you wouldn't have been interested. Something tells me in high school, you were nothing but trouble."

"Damn straight." He grinned. "But I'd have still noticed you."

"I met Craig one night while we were out bowling," I said, forging ahead. I really didn't want to get too caught up in Adam's pretty words because he might change his tune later. "He was with a group of guys in the lane next to us. I was always the best bowler, and he didn't want to lose to a girl." I couldn't help but smile when I thought about it because it had been a fun night. A fun night I wish never happened.

"We actually had this intense competition going on. He got mad when I was beating him. He rolled his ball so fast down his lane that it bounced over into my lane and gave me a strike." I grinned.

Adam smiled, but it didn't reach his eyes. I understood. He knew what was coming. At least some of it.

"Anyway," I said. "After that night, we all started hanging as a group. There wasn't much to do in town so a lot of weekends we would get together at someone's house and watch movies and eat pizza. My best friend had a pool table and a big basement with couches and a TV, so we hung out there a lot. It was always my job to go rent the movies. I have no idea why." I laughed. "I pick the worst movies. They're always so lame." I stuck my tongue out and Adam laughed.

"They would make fun of me for it but still send me the next week. Maybe they secretly wanted to see what horrible thing I'd bring home next."

I realized something as I talked… I realized these memories were attached to Craig, to the feelings I had for him, the feelings that always pulled me back in. But these memories… they weren't even about him. They were about good times I'd spent with my friends, and he just happened to be there.

The thought was a little sobering.

"Rox?" Adam said, reaching over and taking my hand, threading our fingers together and resting them between us on the couch.

"So one night Craig wanted to ride with me to the video store. I was secretly thrilled. He—" I glanced up at Adam, not sure if I could really be honest.

"You can say anything, sweetheart," he whispered.

"He always looked at me like I was the only girl in the room. Like he noticed I was more than friendship material, you know?"

He nodded.

"For a girl who'd never really gotten any attention from guys before, being singled out like that really meant something to me."

"So he went with you," Adam said.

I nodded. "He went every time after that. We'd sing along to the blaring music, roll the windows down even in the winter, and wear hoodies to stay warm. Sometimes we'd eat Fritos out of a giant bag. We were friends… but there was more between us, you know? We had this chemistry. It was almost like we were magnets always being pulled together, even in a room full of people."

"Sounds intense," he rumbled, stroking his thumb over the back of my hand.

"Yeah," I said, thinking about it. "It was. It was fun and light… but underneath it all, it was very intense. Sometimes even our friends would comment on the chemistry that seemed to pulse between us. Looking back, I see how dangerous that was… how much power it gave him over me. I wasn't prepared for that at seventeen. It was way too much too fast."

"You loved him."

I nodded, looking away. "I loved him a lot. More than I ever realized you could love someone."

This heaviness descended upon my chest. It sat just below my ribs like a carnivorous pit in my stomach. Loving someone so much like that… it was consuming. I used to lie in bed at night and worry about what would happen if it ever went away, how I would live without that kind of connection with someone.

My fears turned into my nightmare in so many ways.

I felt Adam's stare but still couldn't bring myself to look at him. I mean, I can't imagine what he was thinking, to hear the girl he'd just said he wanted had been so in love with someone else… to hear her tell him about all the best times we had.

I cleared my throat and kept talking. Now that I had started, it was like I couldn't stop. "I finally got to go to a dance. He took me to my senior prom. He missed the prom at his high school so he could bring me to mine. After the after party, we ate Taco Bell at one in the morning, and I wore his baseball hat in the car."

It hurt to remember these things. It was like mourning someone who died. Someone who just wasn't there anymore, someone you genuinely thought would be there forever.

"I was a virgin when we met," I told him. "And I stayed a virgin for about six months after we started dating. We made out constantly. It got pretty heated sometimes, but he never pushed me into anything I wasn't ready for. When I finally asked him…" I flicked my gaze up. "When I told him I was ready, he used protection. He always treated me like I was important."

"This is fucking hard to hear, Rox," Adam said, his voice gravelly.

"It's hard to say," I admitted. "It's hard to feel."

"The thought of you with him, it makes me crazy. I hear what you're saying—hell, I even understand—but then I look at you and I see the marks on your neck… and goddamn it, Roxie, the side of your face is still red. He hit you, didn't he?"

I chewed my lower lip and nodded.

Adam let loose a string of curses and pulled his hand out of mine. He jumped off the couch and paced to the window and stood with his back to me, staring out over the waves. By this time, the sun was going down, sinking behind the water, and the sky was dusky, the room growing dim.

"Maybe I should go," I said, getting up from the couch.

"No," he said but didn't turn around. "Finish."

I hesitated for a long time, but then I started talking again. "Things were good for a while after we started sleeping together. He treated me really good. But it started to change."

"Change how?" Adam asked, still not looking at me.

"Craig's friends liked to party. Everyone knew it. Hell, most everyone in that town liked to party. It was the only way to blow off steam. When he wasn't with me, he was with them a lot. Some of his friends didn't like me because he spent a lot of time with me. I think they were jealous."

I stood up from the couch and paced to the other side of the room, careful to give Adam space. "Craig started drinking. A lot. He started using drugs. I don't know what kind. I never asked. When we'd go out with friends as a group, he'd drink beforehand. He'd scrutinize what I was wearing. Sometimes he'd throw a fit and tell me I was dressed too provocatively. Sometimes when we were out, he'd yell at other guys he said were checking me out. When we played pool, he'd stand behind me when I bent over the table so no one else could check out my ass."

Adam grunted. I didn't know what that meant and I didn't ask.

"We started fighting. He grew distant. He'd come around smelling like a brewery, and he'd say the most awful things to me. I'd get angry and hurt, but then he'd sober up and apologize. He'd take me in his arms and tell me how sorry he was, that he loved me, and that he needed to get the hell away from his friends and all their influence.

"I was an idiot," I said, knowing it was true. "I loved him so much that I wanted to forgive him. I thought everything would go back to the way it was."

"It didn't," Adam said.

"No. It never did," I echoed. "We spent maybe one good year together. The rest of these years have been nothing but pain and heartache."

"Rox," Adam said, the word etched in pain.

"I threatened to break up with him, more times than I can count. But by then, he'd owned a piece of me, a piece I thought I needed. I'd distanced myself from some of my friends. I didn't see them nearly as much, and I didn't confide in anyone about our fighting and his drinking because I was terribly ashamed. Ashamed that I could be with someone who treated me so horribly. And also, if I'm being totally honest, I wanted to protect him. I loved him, even though I shouldn't have. I still loved him. I didn't want anyone to think badly of him."

I wish I'd known then what I knew now.

"I thought the old him was still in there, but now I know he'd lost himself in the bottle and in whatever drugs he was taking. One night he came to me, told me how messed up he knew he was and how badly he wanted to change. He asked me to move away with him, for us to get out of that town and start a new life. We had already graduated, and I figured I could transfer the college credits I already had to wherever we went. I thought this would be the solution to all our problems. So we moved here, to Myrtle Beach. I was supposed to go to college. He was going to get a job. Things were supposed to be good."

"He couldn't get out of the bottle, could he?" Adam muttered.

"No. Things were better for about a month. Then he fell in with a party crowd. He started using, drinking, and cheating on me. I was so confused and hurt. All this time, I'd thought my love for him would be enough, but it never was. And now I was here, completely isolated with no one to turn to. I packed my stuff one night and put it in the car. That the was the night he started hitting me."

Adam slapped a hand on the window and pressed his fingers into the glass until I could see his knuckles turn white. I decided to hurry up and finish, details be damned.

"College kind of fell to the side, and I got a job at the Mad Hatter. It seemed like we always needed money, that Craig always owed someone something. Stripping paid good."

"He was fucking whoring you out."

"No," I said. "He actually hated the stripping, he was too possessive to even appreciate the money. He told me I was trash and a whore. He used it as an excuse to cheat on me more. He said if I could get naked for other men, then he could sleep with other women."

I took a deep breath. "We were off and on for like the last year. We spent six months apart. I thought we were over, I was starting to breathe again, but then he pulled me back in. There's no excuse for it. I was stupid and naïve. But I'm not anymore. I broke it off for good right before I moved in with Harlow. I hadn't seen him since that night in the bar, but then he started coming around again."

"Do you still love him?" The question ripped from Adam's throat like it hurt to ask. His shoulders were tense, and I had yet to see his face since he moved away from me.

I thought about the question, letting the silence linger because I wanted Adam to hear the real answer. I didn't want to just give him a swift denial. I wanted him to *know*.

"A piece of me will always belong to Craig," I replied. "He was my first love, and I'll never be able to forget that."

Adam leaned his head against the glass.

"But that piece, it's a very small part of my heart, and I don't love him anymore. I stopped loving him a long time ago. I realized the only thing I missed was the way things used to be back when I was seventeen. I could never love someone who hurts me the way he does."

Silence fell around us like a heavy covering of wet snow in the middle of a winter storm. And now he knew. Adam knew the ugly truth of how I stayed with a man who hurt me. He knew how I let it go on and never told a soul. I spared him the ugly details of the holes in the wall from when Craig would go into a fit of rage and punch everything in sight. I didn't tell him how I used to lie in bed at night and cry because I knew Craig was out somewhere sleeping with another woman. I didn't tell him how the smell of alcohol made me panicky, how I was frightened of drunk men. I didn't tell him how ashamed I was and always would be of myself.

The room was dark now. The only light in the room was from the glare of the moon off the ebony waves of the sea. I could make out the shapes of furniture in the room and the solid figure Adam made standing in front of the window, but nothing else.

The longer the silence went on, the sicker I began to feel inside. The pain was incredibly hard to bear. I couldn't really blame Adam for his reaction. I told myself this was how it would be. In a way that only made it hurt worse. I *knew* it would be this way, yet I was still here pouring it all out for him to reject.

When would I ever learn that opening up to anyone was a terrible idea?

When my chest grew so tight it was hard to breathe, I knew I had to leave. I could go down to the gate and have the guard call me a cab. I just hoped this little confession of mine didn't cost me my job. I still needed it.

My bag was lying on the floor beside the sofa, and I crept over and picked it up. I glanced at Adam one last time, feeling my heart constrict, and then walked toward the door.

It was the pain of that moment that taught me something. All those nights years ago when I would lie in bed and cry because I was so afraid I'd never love anyone like I had Craig… I was wrong.

This pain I was feeling, the hurt that threatened to break me in two… I knew it. It was like an old coat I couldn't get rid of. I'd felt it when Craig and my relationship went down the crapper. And every time he showed up and hurt me, I felt it again.

But it wasn't Craig that made me feel this way tonight.

It was Adam.

It was the sting of rejection. It was the hope I'd held inside that he might be able to understand and not see me differently.

I thought he might be able to love me anyway.
He didn't.

But that hadn't stopped me for falling for him. So now here I was, once again in love with someone who didn't love me in return.

20

Adam

I stared at the waves, not really seeing them as she spoke. Roxie had something in common with them. Her life for the past several years had been consistently filled with highs and lows.

And her lows were really low.

I couldn't look at her. I was afraid she might see. I was a man, a self-admitted alpha male. I owned a sports car, a motorcycle, and a strip club. There wasn't much in this life I couldn't handle. I'd been through a serious sports injury that changed my life, four divorces, and building a business.

This was different.

I didn't know how to handle the shitty treatment Roxie had endured. I didn't know how to keep the rage that was bubbling up within me from spilling out. I understood the vulnerability I saw hidden in the depths of her eyes. I understood why it was rare that I ever saw her drink.

I was angry with myself for giving her a job as a stripper, a job for which she was ridiculed and treated like shit at home. A job she took to pay the bills of a deadbeat she somehow felt responsible for.

I knew strippers had bad reps. Hell, I even understood why. It was one of the reasons I didn't date my dancers. Ever. The jealousy meter that was deep down inside me would have blown up at the thought of my woman showing her stuff to other men. Hell, Roxie wasn't even mine and sometimes it was damn hard to watch her strip.

Even still. Strippers were just people. Just women who were doing what they needed to do to pay the bills. I had one putting herself through med school, another supporting her kid because her deadbeat boyfriend walked out on her. Stripping not only paid well, but she spent all day with her kid, then worked while he was in bed. Who the hell was I to judge what someone else did to pay the bills?

In my club, the strippers were shown respect. Period. If I saw anything different, the offender was tossed on his ass with a one-way ticket to never come back.

It fucking killed me that Roxie had been living with such a clump nugget.

It fucking killed me that I had never known.

Sure, I knew he wasn't the best guy. I'd heard rumors of her getting into arguments with him on the phone backstage. But I brushed it off, looked the other way. Roxie was always smiling, always running her mouth… She always had a smile for me.

It was all a cover-up.

Why hadn't I seen past it?

That night I spent on her couch was the first I heard he abused her. I was horrified, but they were already over. He was gone. The one time he showed his face, I beat his ass… I wished I'd killed him.

But I knew now.

And I was never—*never*—going to stand by and watch her get dragged back into that life again.

But I was still left with the question I just didn't know the answer to.

How?

How was I going to handle the anger I felt? The rage, the regret? How was I going to see that vulnerable look in her eyes and not remember exactly where it came from?

I heard a soft sound behind me, pulling me out of my all-encompassing thoughts. I heard the telltale rattling of all the shit in that sack she carried around.

She was leaving.

How long had I stood here in silence?

How long had she waited for me to say something… anything?

I spun and raced across the room as Roxie turned the handle on the front door. She was pulling the door open when I made it to her side. I reached around her and flattened my palm on the wood, pushing it until it latched. She didn't turn around; her head remained bowed.

I slid my palm down, aware of her watching, and turned the lock. The click of it sliding into place reverberated throughout the quiet room.

"You're not going anywhere, sweetheart," I rumbled in her ear.

"I can't do this," she whispered. The intensity in the air around us was thick, so thick I could cut it with a knife.

"Do what?" As I spoke, I slid the white bag off her shoulder and dropped it on the floor.

"I can't get hurt by you, Adam," she whispered. "Just let me go."

"Never."

I laid my hand on her shoulder and slowly spun her around. She looked up at me through shimmering tears.

Placing my hands beneath her arms, I lifted, sliding her up the door until we were face to face, eye to eye. Her legs came up to wrap around my waist, and I flattened my palms on either side of her.

"I'm not ever letting you go," I whispered, staring straight into her eyes. "I love you."

A single tear trickled out and trailed down the curve of her cheek. She squeezed her eyes shut, like it was something she didn't want to hear.

But she was going to hear me.

The question that haunted me through our entire conversation just found its answer. The way to live with the anger, the hurt, and the sickness of knowing what she went through was to channel it. I would channel all those feelings into the love I felt for her, the love that had been growing since the day we met.

I couldn't make up for what he did to her. I couldn't ever take away the scars and pain she would always have.

But I could make sure her future was better than her past.

I could give her the love she wanted all those years ago and never got.

I could love Roxie like that. Like she was the only woman in the entire world.

It would be easy.

Because she is. Roxie was the only woman in my entire universe.

"Look at me," I said softly. When her eyes focused on mine, I told her again. "I love you," I whispered. "I've loved you for a long time. I'm so sorry it took me so long to figure it out."

"Adam," she whispered, her voice quivering.

I shook my head. "I know they're just words, honey. I know you've heard them before. But will you give me a chance to prove them? To show you just how much I mean them?"

She brought her hand up and cupped my face, and I pressed my cheek into her trembling palm. "I was leaving," she said.

I chuckled. "I locked the door. You're not going anywhere."

"Adam," she whispered again. My name on her lips was beautiful.

"Tell me you'll be mine, Rox."

She hesitated. I saw the doubt in her face; I saw the war behind her eyes. She wanted to say yes, but she was afraid of what it would cost her.

"Don't answer me," I told her. "I only want you to give me an answer when you know for sure."

Her chest expanded when she breathed in, and her breasts pushed against me. My groin tightened. I wanted inside her so badly my vision was starting to blur.

"Stay the night with me. In my bed. In my arms," I prompted. I prayed to God this answer was more definitive. If I saw any doubt on her face for this one, I'd probably have to ice my balls.

"Yes," she whispered.

"Yes?" I asked, wanting to make sure I heard her right.

She nodded and gave me a shy smile.

I groaned and crushed our mouths together.

Before I could let myself get carried away, I pulled back and pinned her with another stare. "I'm not talking about just sleep."

A slow smile curved her lips. "I know."

I kind of felt like a choir began signing in perfect harmony when she said those words.

I kissed her again, this time delving my tongue into her mouth and swirling it with hers. We melded together like two ice cubes melting over a flame. My dick was so hard I thought the zipper on my pants might burst, and I was momentarily thankful her legs were around my waist because if she felt how desperately I wanted her, she might be alarmed.

Roxie slid her hands around my neck and pulled me just a little bit closer. My chest rumbled with satisfaction, and I kissed her deeper. One of my hands spanned her ribcage, and I could feel the heat of her skin even through her clothes.

I couldn't even remember the number of times I imagined what it would be like to be with her like this. It was like a fantasy come to life.

I stepped back, pulling her away from the door and walking through my dark apartment. Thankfully, I knew the place well and was able to navigate even as we kissed. The bedroom door was pulled around, and I kicked it open. The curtains on the wall-to-wall window were still open and the moonlight filtered in, casting a silver glow over the room. I sat Roxie on the end of the bed and moved away to slide open one of the windows. The ocean breeze filtered in, bringing with it the scent of the salty sea. The sound of the waves crashing against the shore filled the room with a rhythm that could only be found in nature.

I didn't bother closing the curtains. No one could see in anyway, not that anyone was out on the beach at this hour. Besides, I liked the way the moonlight shimmered on her skin.

At the edge of the bed, I dropped down on my knees, slid the heels off her feet, and shoved them aside. Her skirt was short, showing of her legs, toned from all the dancing she did. I took a moment to rake my fingertips up her outer calf and over her knee.

I took her hand and stood, pulling her along with me so we were standing in the darkened room, facing each other. I cupped her face softly and captured her lips while dragging my fingers through the long strands of her hair. Letting my fingers continue down, I grasped the hem of her lacy top. With one tug, the top slid up and she lifted her arms so I could pull it off her completely. The silky feel of the tank top beneath it slid under my hands like water, and I pulled one of the little straps down and nipped at her shoulder.

Roxie made a sound of pleasure and tipped her head back, so I repeated the action. Her neck was exposed with her position and I couldn't help but look at the area where the fingerprints marred her creamy skin.

That motherfucker tried to choke her. He put his filthy hands around her neck and squeezed.

Rage intruded on the moment, making my body tense. Roxie sensed it and started to shift her body, to close in on herself.

I grasped her hip and held her in place to trail a line of feather-light kisses across the bruised flesh, pouring all that rage into the pleasure I wanted her to feel.

Her body relaxed again, and I smiled against her throat.

In seconds, I had the silky tank off and was reaching for the zipper on the back of her skirt. I couldn't wait to feel her body against mine, to see her completely bare.

As the zipper began to slide down, Roxie pulled back slightly, placing her hands on my chest, silently telling me to stop.

"Adam?" she asked, her voice unsure.

"What, sweetheart?" *Oh shit, she's changed her mind. How the fuck am I going to keep my hands off her?*

"There's something I need to tell you."

21

Roxie

He said he loved me.

Even after everything, he said he loved me.

I desperately wanted to believe him, especially because I'd fallen for him too. It was something I could barely say to myself, and thank God he didn't seem to want me to say it back, at least not right away.

Loving someone was the scariest thing a person could do. It made you vulnerable in ways I never knew it could. And he was right. I needed him to prove the words. I needed him to show me. Maybe then I would be able to say them back.

I could barely think about that now, though. I could scarcely think at all. Kissing Adam was thrilling. My entire body raced with awareness when he touched me, when his tongue brushed against mine.

Little tingles of excitement echoed through my limbs as my body relaxed and readied itself for more. The ache in my center spread lower, down into my panties, where it seemed my heartbeat could be felt strongest. I throbbed for him. I wanted him to touch me there so badly that my inner muscles kept clenching in anticipation.

Adam moved like an expert, the way he kissed, the way he caressed, the way he knew exactly how to remove my clothes…

He was experienced. Far more experienced than I.

When I announced I needed to tell him something, the tension in the room seemed to skyrocket. Adam withdrew his fingers from the zipper at my waist and ran a hand over the top of his head.

"Tell me." His voice was strained, and I knew stopping like that was difficult for him, but I was suddenly so intensely nervous. What if I didn't please him?

"You're…" I began, not really sure how to say it. "You…"

He nodded, encouraging me.

I sighed. "There's only been one before you. Before tonight."

Please let him get my meaning.

Understanding dawned in his eyes. "You've only been with one guy before?"

I sank my teeth into my lower lip and nodded.

He grinned like he'd won the lottery.

Didn't he understand this wasn't good news? "My experience is very limited. I might not be what you want."

Rich, rumbly laughter filled the space and overcame the sound of the ocean outside. "You're exactly what I want," he murmured. Adam traced a finger over the lacey edge of my bra. "There's no need to be nervous with me, Roxie. I'm going to take care of you."

"But what about you?" I worried.

He took my hand and moved it to his bulging crotch, rubbing it up and down the rigid length. "I think it's safe to say I'm taken care of."

I reached for the buttons on his shirt, undoing them one by one, moving just a little bit faster with each one. When his shirt was open, I noticed it was still tucked into the dress pants he was wearing. I wanted to see his chest. I wanted to touch it all. I pushed my hands beneath the fabric. I felt like I was opening a present on Christmas morning, and I was too impatient to take my time.

Adam pulled the tails of his shirt out of his waistband and shrugged the shirt onto the floor. His bronzed skin tone glowed in the light of the moon, and I leaned forward and pressed a kiss to his chest, right above his heart.

Adam sighed and his fingers threaded into my hair, holding my lips hostage on his skin. My tongue slid out and across his smooth chest, dipping low until it brushed over his hardened nipple. I sucked it into my mouth and rolled it around with my tongue.

At the same time, I reached for the buckle on his pants. All the clothes between us seemed like such a barrier. I had his pants undone by the time he untangled his hands from my hair. I pulled back and he started kissing me again, at the same time unzipping the skirt and pushing it down to my ankles.

When I was standing before him in only my bra and panties, he stepped back, his eyes gazing over my body hungrily. "You're the most beautiful woman I've ever seen."

I looked away, blushing, but he put a finger beneath my chin and lifted my face. "Don't do that," he murmured. "Don't look away. I mean it."

I grasped his hand and pressed a kiss to his palm. It seemed ironic for me to be bashful all of the sudden. I mean, I was a stripper. Of course, getting naked in front of strangers was a lot different than baring it all in front of someone I truly cared about.

At the club, I was stripping, showing my skin, and basically just doing a job. It didn't really matter that I had very little actual sexual experience. Men didn't care. They only wanted to see me shake it. Turns out I was pretty good at that.

When I was dancing, I separated myself from it. Just because I was getting almost naked didn't mean I was showing all of myself. There were a lot more parts of me—more important, more vulnerable—and those parts I kept hidden.

But not here.

Not now.

I was baring everything to Adam. I'd let him past my skin. I was showing him everything beneath my curves and flesh.

I was vulnerable to him in ways I could never be at the club.

Yet, he called me beautiful.

During my internal revelation, he quickly pushed off his pants and kicked them away. My eyes went immediately to the massive bulge in his tight boxer briefs. They were black and hugged his hips and thighs like they were custom tailored just for him.

He was so hard that his tip jutted out his waistband, giving me a little peek of his smooth, bulbous head.

I wanted to feel him, to see him. I reached out, hooking my fingers in the thick band of the underwear. Adam's hand covered mine, and he shook his head. "You first."

I frowned and he laughed. "Don't you worry, sweetheart. You'll get your turn."

Adam lifted me like I was nothing but a feather and draped my body across the bed. His large frame came over me, straddling my hips. My breasts fit perfectly in the palms of his hands, and he took full advantage, rubbing against the lacey cups.

My nipples began to ache, pressure building in them, begging for more. I arched my back to give him greater access, so he reached beneath me and unhooked the material on his first try. The garment was flung somewhere into the shadows of the room, and Adam took the fullness into his hands and squeezed gently, holding them up, and bent over to lavish kisses between them.

I purred low in my throat as he suckled the hardened pebbles, pinching them between his fingers and kneading the flesh as he sucked.

His hands and mouth worked simultaneously, and moisture slicked the insides of my panties, drenching them and making my hips swivel around atop the mattress.

Eventually, Adam moved lower, kissing his way across my abs and down near the waistband of my undies. My body stiffened automatically when he swept the fabric off my legs and pushed them wide to settle between them.

"Relax," he murmured. "I'm not going to hurt you." His words were accompanied by the gentle probing of his fingers along my folds. I shuddered, my knees starting to shake.

The groomed, wiry curls at the center of my body seemed to intrigue him as he played with them, pulling his fingers through their middle.

When he lowered his head, like he meant to taste me, I stiffened again. He looked up at me from between my thighs. "What's the matter, sweetness?" he murmured.

"I…" I began as he slid a finger down my slippery slit.

"You don't like this?"

I shuddered.

"'Cause it seems like you do."

"No one's ever…" I murmured as my hips thrust up, seeking his hand once more.

Adam stilled. When I didn't feel his fingers, I opened my eyes wide.

"Are you telling me no one's ever tasted you?"

I shook my head, nervous. My ex never did this. He said he didn't like it. He said the place between my thighs wasn't for his face, only his cock. I'd just assumed no respectable man went down there on a woman. I assumed it was taboo.

Apparently, I was terribly wrong.

"I am one lucky bastard," he muttered and settled himself more thoroughly between my thighs.

"But…" I started, feeling completely self-conscious. What if he didn't like it? There had to be a reason my ex never went down there. Maybe there was something wrong with me.

"You're going to love this. I promise." I felt his fingers part my folds, cool air brushing over the newly exposed flesh. A single finger swirled in my heat, teasing my entrance. "So wet," he crooned as my head fell back against the mattress.

His finger slid into me and I groaned. He moved slowly at first, in and out, dragging that finger along my slit like it was exploring some great unknown. I felt the heat of his stare as he studied me down there and the hot breath he occasionally blew across my swollen bud.

My hips started to swivel, dancing to the pace he set, and then he had two fingers inside me and I felt his lips close around my clit. My body shivered and my legs felt like Jell-O against the mattress. I filled my hands with the blanket on either side of me as the sensation of his mouth and his touch stole over my senses.

My body rose higher and higher; his fingers moved faster and faster. The thickness of his tongue seemed to travel everywhere, not missing a single inch of the place no one else had given so much attention.

I whimpered his name, unsure I could take much more, and his fingers left me. I cried out, feeling empty as his hands wrapped around my hips.

The next thing I knew, his mouth was on me once more and his tongue surged into my body. I started to moan as release washed over me, and Adam licked up, applying the most delicious pressure on the swollen bud.

Bright light exploded behind my eyes and my hips surged off the bed. The orgasm went on and on, and he ate me through the entire thing. He acted like a starving man devouring his only meal.

When I thought I couldn't take any more and my entire body shook like a leaf, Adam lowered my hips back onto the bed and came over me. I glanced up at him through lust-heavy eyes, and he smiled.

I reached for the waistband on his boxers and pushed at them. Adam left me, standing beside the bed, and discarded them totally. His proud member jutted out from his body and caused my eyes to widen. He was huge. I wondered if I would be able to wrap my hand around him and if my fingers would touch.

His balls were heavy and full, and I imagined what they might feel like in the palm of my hand.

Adam reached into the drawer beside his bed and tossed a couple foil packs on the pillow near my head. He ripped one open with his teeth, and I watched with rapt attention as he rolled the condom over his impressive girth.

Part of me was a little sad I hadn't gotten to touch it yet.

I reached for him, but he evaded me. "If you touch me right now, I'll never make it inside you," he rumbled. "I *need* to be inside you."

"I don't think you're going to fit," I blurted out, then slapped a hand over my mouth.

What the hell did I say that out loud for?

Adam threw back his head and laughed. "Oh, I'll fit, sweetheart. That body of yours was made just for me."

He climbed between my legs and settled there. I could feel his bulging head at my entrance. Nerves skittered along my spine. I was worried he wouldn't like it, and I was genuinely concerned he wouldn't fit.

Adam took my face in his hands, looking deep into my eyes, and all worry floated away. He kissed me slow and soft, turning my body to putty.

And then he slid home.

One long, hard thrust brought our bodies together.

Pain was sharp and sudden, and I sucked in a breath. A vein in Adam's neck pulsed as he held himself still over me.

"I'm sorry I hurt you, sweetheart," he said, the effort of holding still clear in his tone. "You're so tight…" He groaned.

I breathed through the twinge of pain as my body stretched around him and coated his shaft with my juices.

Soon there was no pain, only pleasure. In search for more, I swiveled my hips tentatively, and he moaned. I rocked against him again. He looked down at me with a passion-laced stare.

"You feel good," I whispered.

He started to move, to slip in and out of me. My insides stretched around him, and the throbbing of his cock was the center of my world. Tension built in the air, and both of us started moving faster, both of us searching for release.

"Fuck," he growled, "I'm not going to last."

"I don't want you to," I answered as I lifted my hips to match his pace.

He started pounding in me. My legs fell to the sides, and I gripped his biceps, unable to do anything but let the sensation of being loved by him roll over my body.

Adam plunged deep inside me and his arms began to shake. "Now, sweetheart," he whispered, then started pulsating against my walls.

The orgasm crashed over me like the waves in the distance, and I clung to him as we both fell over the edge of bliss. When it was over, Adam collapsed on top of me, supporting his weight on his elbows and kissing the inside of my throat.

"That was the best," he said. "I swear to God."

I giggled as he rolled off me and stared up at the ceiling. He reached between us and took my hand, linking us together as the sound of the ocean filled the room and the scent of our sex lingered in our noses.

I thought I'd enjoyed sex before… but it had been nothing compared to this. Adam was the man everything else in my life would now be measured against.

Nothing else would ever stand a chance in hell.

I was left there with thoughts sneaking into my bliss. Thoughts I didn't want, but couldn't stop. He was the standard now, *my* standard… What if I wasn't his?

"Can I ask you something?" I whispered. Nerves knotted my stomach, but still I had to know.

"Anything," he replied, turning so we were face to face among the pillows.

I smiled, momentarily forgetting the question because he was just so beautiful to me. He'd probably laugh if I told him that.

When I didn't continue speaking right away, he smiled at me softly and pulled the sheet up, tucking it around my bare skin, and then pushed a few rogue strands of hair out of my face. "I love you," he whispered.

I closed my eyes and let those words wash over me. Craig used to tell me he loved me, and it had been thrilling. It made me feel special.

But when Adam said the words…

It made me feel whole.

And it brought me back to the question I needed to ask. "Do you see me different now that you know?"

"Know what, sweetheart?" he murmured, brushing my hair back once more.

I almost told him to forget it because the way he was looking at me was a good enough answer. Yet when the after-sex glow faded, I would still want to know.

"Now that you know all the things I let him do to me."

"You're afraid I think less of you," he said.

I nodded. Of course I was. I knew the kind of stereotype that went with women in bad relationships, women who allowed men to treat them like trash. We were weak; we were insecure and scared. We didn't have enough self-respect to get the hell out, or maybe deep down, we liked being treated like shit.

I didn't think I could stand it if Adam thought of me that way.

"I'm in awe of you, sweetheart," Adam said. "I see a woman who is too strong for her own good, who has the capability of loving so unconditionally that she did so at her own detriment. You loved that asshole in spite of himself. You loved him when he didn't deserve it. Your loyalty astounds me. The fact you stayed true even after you shouldn't have doesn't make you weak, honey. It makes you strong."

"But I let him hurt me," I whispered, tears filling my eyes. I'd never thought about it that way before. I had loved him unconditionally. It just wasn't enough.

"You got caught up in a shitty situation. You were fucking seventeen. You didn't know any better.

By the time you did, you were in so deep it probably felt impossible to get out." Adam reached out and stroked the side of my cheek. "But you did. You got out. And now you're here with me."

"Most men wouldn't want to hear about the number an ex did on a woman they were in bed with."

He smirked. "Sweetheart, I'm not most guys. I'm awesome."

I giggled. "Yeah. You are."

"And I'd be a damned hypocrite if I got mad you were in someone else's bed before mine. I've been married four times. Four failed marriages. Frankly, I'm shocked you'd be here with me."

"I guess we both have a past," I whispered.

"We both have a future too." He leaned forward and kissed me, a lingering caress that touched me deep inside. "I don't give a shit about your past, Rox. It's your future I'm after," he murmured against my lips.

A fluttering filled me up inside, making me feel light and jittery. I never thought I'd feel this way again… I never realized the second time around would be even better than the first.

I lifted the sheet and slid beneath it, bringing my body up against his. Both of us were still lying on our sides, facing the other. I draped my arm around his side and pulled him just a little bit closer. My breasts flattened against his chest, and I purred a little with the skin-on-skin contact.

Adam palmed the back of my head and pulled me so he could suck my lower lip into his mouth. My nails dug into his back, and we began kissing hungrily.

He rocked his hips toward me and his hardness poked me.

Even though we'd just made love, my body wanted him again. The feel of his stiff cock thrusting against me while his tongue delved into the depths of my mouth had fresh moisture slicking the inside of my thighs and the center of my body.

I lifted my leg and threw it up over his hip, inviting him inside.

The swollen, silky head of his penis probed at my entrance, seeking access inside my body. I was so wet he slid along my slit, unable to plunge inside.

I moaned because he felt so incredible, and I wiggled my hips, trying to help him find his way.

Adam untangled our lips and groaned. "Please tell me you're on the pill," he panted, his hips still thrusting against me.

"I am," I replied, tilting my hips upward.

"I swear to God I'm clean, sweetheart," he said as the tip of his head found my hole.

I gasped. The feeling of his skin on my skin was incredible. He was so smooth and tight. I desperately wanted him to push inside, to fill me up.

I made a little sound and rocked against him.

Adam grabbed my hip and stilled me, holding himself poised at my entrance. "Look at me, Roxie."

My eyelids fluttered open, and I connected with the dark pools of his eyes. He was so close I could see the effort it took for him to not plunge inside me.

"Tell me it's okay," he rumbled.

I tightened the leg thrown over his hip and pushed myself closer. "I want you inside me, Adam. Right now. Just you. Nothing between us."

One hard thrust brought him in deep. Both of us groaned, and I splayed my palm against his lower back and pressed him closer. I wanted him as deep as he could get.

He murmured my name, and I wiggled down, ducking my head against his chest. Adam wrapped an arm around me, holding me tight as he began to move. The fluid motion of his hips, the rocking of his cock inside me, made my brain feel fuzzy. I'd never had sex in this position before, but I loved it. I was completely against him, wrapped up in him. The steely length of his cock lay against my inner wall, and the way it slid back and forth against me built up an incredible pressure inside me.

My fingers curled inward and my nails dug into his skin. I pulled him deeper and he thrust harder.

"Adam," I cried. My body was searching for release, craved it.

"That's it, sweetheart," he answered and pressed his lips against my forehead. "Come for me."

The friction he created by all the rubbing against my inner wall created a spark, and suddenly it burst into a flame. The orgasm lit me up inside. My entire body began to tremble and I bore down on him, pumping my hips against his as ecstasy rolled through me.

I held on to him as the sensation went on and on. Adam made a sound in the back of his throat and thrust into me, holding himself there, rigid and still. I started moving, rocking my hips back and forth.

"Don't stop," he whispered as his body tightened.

Inside me, his head began to pulse, and he crushed me against him. I felt his hot seed pouring out, and I held on as I milked every last drop from his shaft. I loved the feeling of him leaving something inside me, of my body drinking in his essence.

I'd never felt so sated in my entire life.

"Holy fuck," he muttered when breath returned to our bodies.

I pressed a kiss into his chest and snuggled closer. "Don't leave me yet."

A laugh rumbled through him. "Sweetheart, I'm not going anywhere. The feel of you around me is goddamn amazing."

I yawned. The sleep I didn't get the night before was catching up to me and being wrapped up in his warm embrace, feeling so relaxed, was making my eyes grow heavy.

But I didn't want to go to sleep.

I didn't want to miss a single minute with Adam.

"Get some sleep, Rox," Adam said, as if he could read my mind.

"I don't want to," I whined, even as I yawned again.

He chuckled. "Oh, I won't let you sleep long," he promised. "I'm not done with you yet."

I closed my eyes and drifted to sleep with a smile still on my lips.

22

Adam

I pushed myself hard on my morning run, sprinting across the sand beside the water. The force of my step kicked up some sand on my calves, but I ignored it.

Getting out of bed to run at all had been an accomplishment because Roxie was right beside me. Even though I'd had her over and over throughout the night, when I opened my eyes and saw her hair across the pillow and her still slightly swollen lips so close, my cock jackknifed into position. Even though I wanted her again, I didn't reach for her. She was likely already sore, and I didn't want to hurt her.

She'd been hurt enough already.

So here I was out on the sand, trying to run off the worst of my need and anger. And yeah, the punishing pace would only get me back to her faster. I knew the old injury in my knee would probably hate me later for this, but it was a price I would gladly pay.

It was a scorcher, and I wiped my brow with the back of my hand, rubbing away some of the sweat.

Usually, I ran as the sun was just rising, but I was late this morning and the sun was higher in the sky. Last night had been just too fucking amazing.

Roxie was a combination of naughty and nice all tied up into one total package. I had no idea she was so innocent. Her reactions to me and my touch were so honest that I couldn't keep my hands off her. She kept reaching for me. The curiosity in her eyes for my body had me on the verge of orgasm the entire night. I wanted her touch, craved it, but I wanted to satisfy her more.

It became clear the more I touched her that her past experiences with the douche bag had not been that great. He'd been a selfish lover, taking but never reciprocating. I felt sorry she didn't know what she'd been missing, but I was fucking thrilled I was the one to show her.

Even with all the pleasure we found last night, I still couldn't forget the things she told me. I was still so angry, and it terrified me I always would be. Thank God the marks on her neck would fade. There was no way in hell I could look at them forever and not go after him.

And the need to go after that motherfucker was pretty intense.

I sent up silent thanks that I already had a restraining order slapped on his ass for the club. At least while Roxie was there I could breathe a little easier knowing she was safe.

I didn't know what I would do if I saw him. Self-control wasn't my best quality, and when it came to Roxie, I had a feeling I would be a loose cannon. She didn't need that. She needed someone more stable, someone who could keep his shit together and be the rock she never had.

It made me crazy she'd been navigating life all by herself for years while trying to clean up the mess of the man who was too stupid to know what he had.

No more.

I realized that even though I told her I loved her, she never said it back. When I asked her to be mine, her eyes turned wary. But that was okay. I wasn't going to give up on her. On us. I'd wait until she was able to say the words, and they would be even sweeter because I earned them.

My building came into view, towering above the beach farther down the sand. Heat coursed through my body and all the blood went straight into my shorts. Clearly, my intense, punishing run hadn't been enough to dull the desire I felt for her.

I kept running. My gaze followed the line of waves crashing at the shore, and my attention was snagged by someone walking across the sand toward the water.

Her dark hair whipped behind her, tangling in the wind off the water, and she was wearing a too-large white shirt, the sleeves hanging well past her hands.

Roxie.

She was wearing my shirt.

Good God, this woman had a habit of wearing my shit and making it look amazing. Her long, tan legs stretched down to the sand, her feet bare. She was probably naked beneath my button-up.

I picked up the pace.

My eyes never wavered from her as I ran, and I watched as the water rushed up the shore at her feet and she squealed and dashed backward.

I am going to love her 'til the day I die.

She was it for me.

The end.

The beginning.

My everything.

I smiled because I knew she must have found my note.

As if she sensed me, Roxie turned and glanced in my direction. Her body changed when she recognized it was me.

A smile broke out over her face and she started jogging toward me. The tails of my dress shirt trailed behind her and the front plastered against her body.

I slowed my pace when I was almost to her, and she laughed, launching herself at me.

I caught her with ease, and her legs wrapped around my waist.

"I got your note," she said with a grin.

I moved in to kiss her. She squealed. "You're all sweaty!"

"Didn't stop you from leaping into my arms," I drawled.

"You need a shower," she said, a twinkle in her eyes.

Yeah, that got me rock hard. Just the thought of her in the shower with water running down her naked body…

I dropped onto the sand, pinning her beneath me and attacking her lips with mine. She laughed, but it quickly turned into a moan, and her arms slid around my neck to match my kiss with one of her own. I made sure I rubbed my sweaty self all over her front and smooshed her in the sand so her hair got full of it.

"Hey!" she yelled between kisses. "You're making me a mess!"

I pulled back to grin down at her. "Now you need a shower too."

"Good thing I'm already half naked," she purred.

My hand slid up the outside of her leg and my fingers skimmed against the skin where her panties should have been. I felt my eyes grow wide.

"Roxie!" I growled and looked around for prying eyes. "I'm trying real hard not be possessive of you, sweetheart, but you're making it fucking impossible."

"Being possessed by you doesn't seem so bad," she said softly.

"How about being loved by me instead?" I asked, kissing the tip of her nose.

"That sounds even better."

I jumped to my feet and grinned at the sexy mess she was in the sand. She pushed up onto her elbows and grimaced. On impulse, I swept her up in my arms and starting walking toward the stairs that led to my building, her laugh floating behind us the entire way.

23

Roxie

For once in my life, I didn't mind waking up.

With Adam's scent surrounding me, silky sheets beneath my body, and knowing whose arms I slept in, I was frankly thrilled to be awake.

Maybe Adam was the ultimate cure for my all-hate relationship with morning.

I rolled over and reached for him, but the bed was empty. The pillow still bore the indent from his head, but he was gone.

I sat up and pushed the hair out of my face and looked around the room. Also empty. Sunlight streamed through the windows because we'd never bothered to close the curtains. The view was absolutely stunning.

Sunlight sparkled on the ever-moving water, the blue sky stretched on forever, and the white-capped waves slowly rolled in. The air smelled of salt and sea, and I took a deep breath. I couldn't remember the last time I felt so relaxed.

Being here with Adam was incredible. *He* was incredible. He was even more than I imagined.

I wondered if maybe he was in the kitchen making coffee, but then I giggled because Adam didn't make coffee. The one time I saw him attempt it, he caught the pot on fire.

Maybe he'd gone out for coffee.

I flopped back into the pillows and grinned up at the ceiling. I was in Adam's bed. I was naked.

Harlow was never going to believe it when I told her.

I became aware of certain parts of my body, parts that hadn't been utilized in a while. I was stiff and sore. I felt slightly swollen, but it was awesome. I stretched out, wiggling my toes and lifting my arms above my head. I rotated my hips to the side and caught a dark shadow.

Frowning, I looked down.

Then I burst out laughing.

I rolled my head to the side and saw the black Sharpie lying on the table beside the bed. I laughed again and then bounded off the bed and into the adjoining bath.

Adam's apartment was very modern. All dark wood, sleek lines, and chrome fixtures. It was definitely a house a man would live in, but there was nothing cold about it. It was inviting. I loved it here.

I lifted my eyes above the white stone countertop and into the huge mirror. A grin spilt my face.

Adam didn't go without leaving me a note.

On my body.

I brought my finger up and traced the outlined of his hand-drawn message. My heart swelled just staring at the message.

He was down on the beach. I remembered he said he ran every morning.

He could have found a piece of paper or even a napkin.

But he didn't.

He wrote it on my skin.

Right on the inside of my hipbone, in a place only I would see. I loved it. I absolutely loved it. Maybe he was only being silly. Maybe he got a kick out of drawing on me.

But this was so much more to me than marker.

Thank goodness it was permanent because I already worried about it fading away. At least this way it would last a little bit longer.

I traced the image again, letting my finger touch the marks he made, the heart he drew. Craig and I had been together a long time, many years, in fact. It wasn't often he gave me anything. Yeah, when we first started dating, when things were good, he sometimes brought me a rose, and we went out on a couple dates, just the two of us.

I couldn't even begin to count the number of times I woke up and he wasn't there. The number of days he would be out on a binge and never call, never think that maybe I would be worried. It's like I meant so little to him that he never thought of me at all.

He certainly never left me a note.

One time I found a gold necklace in his car… It wasn't mine. He never gave me jewelry. I found out later it was something he had given one of his conquests.

This hand-drawn note wasn't gold. It didn't cost any money, and it would likely fade away in several days…

But it was the best gift I'd ever received.

Adam probably only thought it was a cute way of telling me where he was. And it definitely was that.

But this was a gift. A sign. Proof that he thought of me, that he knew I might wonder where he was when I woke to an empty bed. It was his way of telling me he was coming back, that I would be in his head while he was away.

This was everything.

I needed to see him. I wanted to feel his arms around me. With one last smile at the note on my skin, I raced out of the bathroom and grabbed his white dress shirt off the floor where it fell last night.

Hastily, I yanked it on and went outside to find the access to the beach.

Going outside to meet him in nothing but his shirt earned me a sweaty kiss and a dunk in the sand. I'd have to remember that for the future because I wanted more of sweaty Adam.

He carried me the entire way up to his condo. I worried about his back, his knees, and his biceps. He rolled his eyes every time I asked him if I was too heavy.

See, this was the kind of stuff I never knew I missed.

I never knew someone could make me feel wanted—small yet strong, weak but brave.

I screeched as we trailed sand through his house and into the bathroom. Once there, I thought he would set me on my feet, but he didn't. He set me on the countertop and then walked to the glass-enclosed shower and turned on the faucet. He wasn't wearing a shirt and his sun-kissed chest glistened with sweat. I had this incredible urge to lick him, to taste him and the salty air all in one.

Without a second thought, he stripped off his running shorts and boxers in one swoop. Since he already discarded his socks and shoes outside, he was totally naked.

Heat simmered in my core and spread, like a flame catching on a puddle of gasoline. He was already hard, and I enjoyed the full view as he prowled across the tile at me. Adam's dark eyes smoldered as he fitted himself between my legs.

He began to unbutton my shirt, exposing my skin inch by inch.

"I know I already told you, but I love your note," I told him, watching as he concentrated so fully on the buttons.

The corner of his mouth curved up and his dark eyes flashed to mine. "Yeah?"

I nodded and put my hands over his, stilling his movement. He looked up. "Thank you, Adam."

He seemed a little taken aback by the sincerity, the true gratitude behind my words. "I thought about writing 'I was here,' but I didn't think you'd think that was very funny."

I grinned. "Have you ever left a note on a girl before?"

"Nope. You're my first." His eyes twinkled.

I liked being someone's first at something.

"What about you, sweetheart?" he asked playfully.

I pushed my palm beneath the open shirt and laid my hand over the drawing. "It's the best thing I've ever been given."

Sorrow passed behind his eyes and the muscles in his jaw ticked. I worried that maybe I'd made too big of a deal out of something he didn't see as such. But then it was gone and he smiled.

I shrugged out of the shirt and let it pool around my waist on the counter. Adam picked me up and I wrapped my legs around his middle. His palms cupped my ass, and I couldn't resist rocking my core against him.

He stepped into the shower. My back was to the water and it rained down over my shoulders and saturated the back of my hair.

"You wash my back, I'll wash yours?" he asked, letting me slide down his body. Just the feel of his hard-on pushing against me was exciting.

"Just don't wash this off, okay? I wanna keep it," I said, pointing at his drawing.

"I'll draw you another one, sweetheart," he said, dropping a kiss to my lips.

"But I want this one."

"Whatever you want," he said and reached up to lean my head back and saturate it with water.

We washed each other under the warm, gentle spray. I got to see and learn his body in ways I hadn't last night.

It was the first time I was able to really touch him freely without him trying to stop me. Once I was clean and rinsed, I slipped around him so he faced the spray. I grabbed the soap and began to wash his broad back, enjoying the way his muscles felt beneath his skin.

When I'd washed everything in sight, I put the soap down and slipped my hands around his waist. I enjoyed the rippled feeling of his abs beneath my fingertips, and I explored him for a long time. Eventually, my hands began to roam south, to the nest of short, neat curls just above his package.

Adam groaned and leaned back a little, closer to my body. Feeling brave, I wrapped my hand around the base of his cock, reveling in the wide thickness. I was right. When I wrapped my thumb and forefinger around him, they didn't touch.

I began to stroke him, to explore him, and the way his body reacted was amazing. It was like he turned to putty in my hands.

But I wanted more. I didn't want to just touch and stroke him. I wanted to taste him as well.

I moved back in front of his body and sank onto my knees before him. I cupped his balls in my hand, testing their weight and fullness. I glanced up from beneath lowered lashes, and the shower water ran down my face and hair.

Our eyes connected and held.

Adam reached out and braced his hands on either side of the shower walls. I held his chocolate gaze as I pulled his cock out toward me, keeping one hand wrapped around the base. Slowly, I took him into my mouth, inch by delicious inch, until I could feel him at the back of my throat.

His hand slid around the back of my head and his fingers delved into the wet strands of hair. I began to move, and his eyes slid closed. Then so did mine.

He was so incredibly smooth and hard, and the feel of him against my tongue, even nudging the back of my throat, was heady. Desire rose up inside me, and I felt my core liquefy, my body readying itself for him.

But I didn't want to stop.

I wanted to suck him until he let go and filled my mouth.

I kept sucking and licking, changing up my pace and occasionally gently scraping my teeth over his shaft.

When his hips started pumping softly into my mouth, I smiled. I knew he was enjoying this.

When his body went rigid and his cock started to jerk, he tried to pull me back, but I refused to let go.

"Rox," he mumbled, trying once more to get me to release him.

I sucked harder and gripped his hips in my hands.

His shout bounced off the bathroom walls, and he pumped into my mouth as his semen slid across my tongue. It was salty and warm, kind of like the beach.

I swallowed it without thinking twice. When I pulled back, I wrapped my hand around him and stroked him carefully a few more times. I loved the way his body shuddered, like he just couldn't get enough.

Then he was shutting off the water and pulling me up. The softest, biggest towel I'd ever seen was wrapped around my body, and he began to dry my limbs.

Once I was mostly dry, he grabbed another towel and hastily rubbed over himself. Adam swept me off my feet and carried me out to the bed, where he laid me across the center and pulled the towel away from my body.

"What are you doing?" I asked, even though I already knew.

"Reciprocating," he replied, spreading my thighs.

We didn't leave the bedroom until much, much later.

24

Adam

For the first time in a long time, I wasn't chomping at the bit to get to work. In fact, I was kind of pissed we had to go. Being alone with Roxie was the only place I wanted to be right now.

Even still, I had a business to run, and since I missed last night, I had shit to make up for.

Although I knew I needed to get my ass in gear, it didn't stop me from sitting back and enjoying the sight of Roxie wiggling her tight ass into the fitted skirt she had on last night.

I couldn't help but notice the way she moved a little stiffly, and I felt guilty because I knew I'd overdone it with the sex. It was just so damn hard to keep my hands off her.

I pushed away from the closet where I was pulling out clothes and snagged her around the waist, towing her against me. She didn't have a shirt on yet, only her bra, and just touching the smooth skin of her waist was enough to turn me on. "You're sore."

She leaned against me, the back of her head resting against my shoulder. "It was worth it."

"Stay here with me tonight."

She laughed. "I don't think that will help with my soreness."

"I just want you here. I want you close. We don't have to have sex."

She turned in the circle of my arms. "No?" Her eyebrow arched. "But what if I want to?"

"I wouldn't turn you down." I smiled.

She stretched up on her tiptoes and kissed me. "'Kay."

"I'll show you a couple more things at the club and make sure everything's straight from last night, but then I gotta head over to Mad Hatter II. I need to check in on the progress and make sure the stock arrived."

"Tonight's my first official night as manager," she said and stepped out of my arms to pick up her tank and pull it on.

"You can call me if you have any problems."

"I'll be fine," she said, picking up her black lace top. She wrinkled her nose at it and tossed it on the bed. Her shapely ass sashayed past me as she went into the bathroom. A few seconds later, she came out wearing the white dress shirt she had on earlier.

I grinned. "What is it with you and my clothes?"

She paused in buttoning it up. "Does it bother you?" she asked, suddenly looking a little shy.

"Hell no," I drawled, moving to help her finish buttoning it. "My closet is your closet. I can't say I like the idea of all the men at the club looking at you in my shirt. It's too fucking sexy."

She laughed. "I have to go home and change. I can't wear the same outfit two days in a row."

I grunted. *Women.* "Get something for tomorrow, then, too so you don't have to go home again."

A funny look crossed her face and her cheeks seemed to pale.

"Are you sick?" I asked, going to her side.

She shook her head and then gave me a smile. "I'm okay. I think I just need some coffee."

"Woman, you know me and coffee is a fire hazard."

That earned me a grin. "I can make it."

"I, uh, don't have a coffee pot."

She gasped. "I cannot stay where there is no access to coffee." The horror on her face was amusing as hell.

"I'll buy you a coffee machine, sweetheart, the best one there is."

"Hmmm." She pretended to consider.

I kissed her silly, making her forget all about the coffee. She swayed when I released her. I smiled smugly. "C'mon, get your stuff. We'll get your coffee on the way to the club."

We took the Roadster this morning because it was hot as hades outside and sitting on the bike was not appealing. Plus, it would make it hard to drink coffee. The little noises she made when her first, second, and third sips passed through her lips gave me an instant hard-on.

Her Mazda was still sitting in the same spot she parked it in the night before, and I had a flashback of her flushed cheeks from her broken A/C. Instead of taking the spot next to her, I pulled the car in front of hers and left the engine to idle.

"What are you doing?" Roxie asked, glancing at me.

"Take my car."

"What? No." She refused, just like I knew she would. She was stubborn with a capital S.

"I will not have you driving around in this heat without A/C," I told her. "You're gonna get sick."

"My place isn't that far from here. I'll be fine," she insisted.

"Yes," I said. "You will be because you'll be in *this* car with the air going."

"Adam." She said my name like it was a threat.

It turned me on.

I pinned her with a hard stare. "I won't have it. What the hell kind of man would I be if I let you drive around like that?"

"The kind I'm used to," she muttered, looking away.

The words pierced me like an arrow to the chest. It wasn't anything to do with me, it wasn't a slam on me, but on every other guy she'd ever known.

"Fuck," I muttered and climbed out of the driver's seat, letting the car idle.

This woman was going to drive me insane.

I stalked around the front end of the BMW and around to the passenger side and wrenched open the door. Roxie was looking at me warily, like she wasn't sure what was going on.

"I shouldn't have said that." She apologized. "You're nothing like any other man I've known."

"You don't have to apologize," I told her, crouching down in the open doorway.

"Yeah. I do. That was bitchy."

"I like me a sassy woman."

She smiled.

I took her hand in mine, holding it in the space between us. "I'm gonna make something clear right here, right now," I said quietly, calmly.

She took note of the no-shit serious tone and her hand tensed in mine.

"I'm the kind of man who takes care of what's his. You make my overprotective instincts go crazy. I'm never going to be a guy who lets you fend for yourself. I'm going to buy you presents. I'm going to fix your shit when it's broken. I'm probably going to bitch about your sexy ass and bra-like shirts. And under no circumstances am I going to sit around with my thumb up my ass and let car mechanics screw you over while I drive around in my BMW. That's not who I am, not with you."

"Adam…" This time my name didn't sound like a threat. It sounded like a promise.

"Get your sexy ass out of the car," I said and gave her a tug. She came willingly. "Think you can handle that?" I asked, looking into her eyes.

"Yeah." Her voice was hoarse. "I can handle that."

I kissed her softly and whispered, "I love you," against her lips. She smiled.

I led her around to the driver's side and held out my hand. "Give me your car keys."

"Why?" she asked cautiously.

"In case there's an emergency and I need to leave."

She fished them out of that endless bag on her shoulder and handed them over. I slid them in my pocket. "I'll see ya when you get back."

I watched her slip into the driver's seat of the Roadster. She seemed nervous.

"I've never driven a car this nice before." She worried, chewing on her lower lip.

"Get used to it." I leaned down in the doorframe.

"You know I don't need presents or fancy cars… All I really want is you."

And that's exactly why I was going to give her everything.

"Call me if you get held up," I said, shutting the door and poking my head through the window to kiss her one last time.

"You're a really good boyfriend," she whispered as I was backing away. Then she gave me a little wave and reversed out of the lot.

I watched until she turned onto the main road. I wondered if she realized what she just said.

I was pretty sure she hadn't meant to call me that. But I was fucking thrilled she did. She hadn't answered my question last night. She hadn't told me yet if she would be mine.

But now she didn't have to.

I already had my answer.

25

Roxie

A slip of the tongue.

It's all it took for me to know how I truly felt.

Boyfriend.

One word.

One seemingly insignificant word.

Adam was so much more than my "boyfriend," but I had no idea how else to classify him.

Keeper of your heart, a voice in my head whispered.

My stomach squirmed with nerves because it felt like too much too soon.

We'd only just started seeing each other. Technically, I guess we still weren't. I never did tell him if I would be his. My subconscious told him, though.

I wondered if he noticed what I called him just before I drove away. I was sure he did, and he didn't correct me. I smiled and turned up the radio.

This car was incredible. It slid over the road like its tires were made of butter. Yet I felt like it owned the road, that it was stable and reliable. The seats were buttery soft leather, the controls on the dash right at my fingertips. It was a convertible two-seater, but it was just too hot to have the top down. The A/C was sinful, and I sighed in appreciation at how cold and crisp it blew out of the vents. My car's air never got this cool, even when it worked.

But even if Adam didn't have a nice car or an apartment on the beach, I would still have fallen for him. He didn't seem to put much value into material things. I think he just liked nice stuff. I couldn't fault him for that because everyone liked nice stuff. And he worked for the things he had; he put in the hours and the late nights. He earned it.

He didn't try to sell his girlfriend into adult films to pay his bills.

I blanched, a sour taste in my mouth. I'd almost forgotten about that little confrontation I had with Craig. But then Adam mentioned tomorrow, and it all came crashing back.

Be at that address day after tomorrow, Roxie. Come dressed like the trashy bitch you are.

It's already a done deal.

Craig expected me to show up at some skeevy address tomorrow and have sex on command. Sex with someone I didn't know. Someone I didn't want to know. Someone who would probably make my skin crawl.

If I had any doubt that I had any love left in my heart for Craig, it was completely gone. I could never love anyone who tried to whore me out. Literally.

I hadn't lied to Adam. In fact, the truth had been hard as hell to say out loud. But I wanted him to know. I wanted to give him all the info before he decided he really did want me.

Craig would always have a little piece of my heart. I think it's like that for all first loves. At least I hoped it was. If not, then I was one twisted bitch.

But I was finally okay with that. I was okay with it because that little piece of me belonged to the Craig I knew when I was seventeen. The guy who wore hoodies in the cold and sang to the radio way too loud and off key. He was the guy who fed me Fritos right out of the bag and the first guy to make my heart flutter beneath my ribs.

That Craig wasn't the same one I knew today. This Craig scared me.

I wondered what he would do when I didn't show up. How angry he would be. What if he took his anger out on Adam and not me? Could I live with myself if Adam got hurt—or worse—because he got caught up in my past?

But I couldn't go. Just the thought of starring in some porn made me want to pull over and vomit. Yeah, Craig mentioned it when we were still together. He brought it up more than once. I always told him he was crazy, and he always sort of laughed it off.

But he hadn't been joking.

One night when he was really drunk and really high, he came home crying. He smelled like cinnamon schnapps, and it made my stomach heave, but even still, I sat with him, close to his side, while he cried about how unworthy he was.

We'd had the same conversation many times.

It didn't matter how many times I told him he was good enough, that he was worth more than he thought… Turns out you can't tell someone their own self-worth. They have to feel it for themselves.

And then he turned desperate. He told me he had a way to get us free of the life we were living, a way to solve all our problems.

If I did just a couple movies, we'd have enough to settle all our debts (our debts = money he owed his dealers), and he could go to rehab, get clean for real, and then we could start a new life. A better life.

I already knew the only better life for me was one without him. I'd known for a long time. I just didn't know how to get out. I didn't know how to get away.

Of course I told him no. I said it as gently as I could. I promised I'd find another way to get him into rehab and out of debt.

He didn't like my answer.

He screamed ugly things at me. The scent of that damned cinnamon schnapps gusted over my face. He told me I had to do it. I didn't have a choice.

I tried to leave.

He hit me.

He hit me more than once.

When he passed out, I snuck out. I slept in my car that night.

Shortly after, I met Harlow. I moved out and months passed.

I thought he'd forgotten about the porn stuff. I should have known better.

The revving of an engine brought me out of the terrible memory. It was close by, and I glanced out the window in the lane beside me, then in the lane to my right. There was no car with a revving engine.

Then I heard it again.

I glanced in the rearview mirror.

A car that looked like a something you would find in a cereal box was riding my bumper so closely that I couldn't see the front end of it at all.

My pulse spiked and adrenaline started to pump through my veins. I squinted down at the speedometer. I was traveling five miles over the speed limit so I wasn't being slow.

Again, I scanned the lanes to my left and right. There was plenty of opportunity to pass me.

Suddenly, the car behind me swerved erratically and sped up beside me. The car was so incredibly close to the side of the BMW, I flinched, bracing for a hit.

What the hell!

I peeked over to get a look at the driver, but he yanked the steering wheel and almost smacked into me. I screamed and jerked the wheel to get away.

The car in the lane beside me laid on their horn as I cut them off.

The matchbox car was now driving in the lane I'd just been in and he was swerving around, coming close, then backing away and repeating the action over and over.

Cars around us were beeping their horns and speeding up to get around the maniac driver.

Every time I tried to pass him, he'd swerve at me again, trying to run me off the road.

Oh my God, he was trying to run me off the road.

I punched the gas and pulled onto the shoulder of the road and drove that way, passing a couple cars illegally and then taking a sharp right-hand turn to avoid my pursuer.

The sound of tires squealing and horns blaring had me looking out the back window. The car had literally cut through the traffic to follow me.

Fed up and scared out of my mind, I slammed on the brakes, jerking the car to a sudden halt. I pulled to the side of the street and sat there.

Let him come.

I was sooo not in the mood for this today.

The matchbox car rolled down the street toward me, almost creeping. It was freaky because I felt like I was being stalked. Hunted.

I hated it.

I rolled my window down just as he slid up beside me.

His window was down too.

He was wearing a hat pulled low over his face, an oversized sweatshirt, and a pair of sunglasses. He lifted his arm, pointing something in his hand at me.

My mouth fell open and I froze.

Was that a gun?

"No!" I shrieked and threw my hands up in front of my face.

The tires screeched as the car jerked to a halt.

Slowly, I pulled my hands away and looked at the man holding out a gun. Even though he was wearing shades, I felt it when our eyes connected.

"Shit," he mouthed.

Then he lowered the gun and sped away.

I collapsed against the seat, breathing like I'd just run a marathon.

That man had tried to run me off the road and then he meant to shoot me!

I don't know what scared him away, why he suddenly changed his mind, but I was grateful.

Trashy

I could be dead right now.

26

Adam

I went through the glove box of Roxie's Mazda. The receipt for the so-called new air conditioner was there. She paid a shit ton of money and they screwed her.

It pissed me off.

I noted the address of the place, then jammed the receipt in my pocket and let myself in the club. Everything looked in order, the place was clean and ready to open tonight.

I went in my office, read through the short but thorough report Cam jotted on a bar napkin, and then checked my messages.

Once I answered the most urgent shit, I palmed the keys to Roxie's car and locked up the club.

The repair place was about ten miles down the road, so I pulled out onto the main drag and stopped immediately at a red light. I'd been in this car for all of two minutes, with the windows down, and I was already sweating and miserable.

It pissed me off even more.

When the light turned green, I gassed it, hoping to get some airflow in this tomb. As I went through the intersection, I noted a red sports car pull out behind me. I might not have noticed, but it was a sweet ride and I liked sweet rides.

I got an even better look at it when it pulled up right behind me.

I got this feeling in my gut. It wasn't a good one. I kept driving down the road, glancing at the car every few seconds. It was definitely following me.

Since this was Roxie's car, that meant whoever that asshole was back there probably thought they were following her.

Oh, hell no.

I jerked the wheel into a nearby parking lot. Ironically, it was an auto repair shop. I didn't bother pulling into a parking spot.

The red car pulled into the lot behind me, rolling across the pavement toward the Mazda. I unhooked my seatbelt and sprang out of my driver's seat. Red tinged my vision and my teeth gritted together.

This better not be who I thought it was.

I'd fucking beat his ass.

Then I'd run him over.

Leaving the car door open, I rose to my full height, letting the pumping adrenaline fuel my muscles, and walked toward the car traveling closer.

I stared at the windshield where I knew the driver sat. The glare of the sun on the glass made it impossible to see who was driving. I didn't really care. Whoever this was needed to know following around Roxie was a giant hell no.

The car slowed as I marched toward it. Challenge was clear in my presence. Then the car shifted into reverse and backed away.

I started running.

The tires peeled, leaving behind a little cloud of smoke as the car sped down the street, hung a left, and drove out of sight.

I was kind of sorry he left in such a hurry.

I got back in the Mazda and drove the rest of the way to the repair shop. Those fuckers didn't stand a chance. I parked the car right at the entrance in a spot that wasn't a parking spot at all and stalked into the service center.

I pulled out the receipt and slapped it down on the counter. Everyone in the place jumped and sat up at attention.

I snarled as I spoke. I told them how very unhappy I was that my woman got ripped off and was sweating her ass off in the southern heat.

Then I made sure they knew just how unhappy I was.

By the time I slammed out of the place, Roxie was getting a brand new air-conditioner, an oil change, and a set of brand new tires.

For free.

It would be done tomorrow.

If it wasn't, this place would be shut down by the end of next week.

Fuckers.

I took a cab back to the club.

Who the fuck had been following Roxie? And why?

27

Roxie

I was still shaking when I pulled into a nearby gas station. It wasn't the one I usually stopped at on my way home, and I chose that one on purpose.

I needed a few extra minutes to calm my racing heart. I knew Harlow was most likely at home, and I didn't want to get there looking as freaked out as I felt.

Maybe it was just a joke.

Maybe it had been a horrible, horrible joke.

It wasn't, a voice inside me hissed.

I decided, since I was there, to top off the tank. Technically, Adam didn't need gas, but I figured if I was going to drive his car, the least I could do would be to replace the gas.

When I was done, I drove the car forward into a spot by the door. I walked inside to pay for the gas and decided to grab something cold to drink. Maybe the icy cold water would jolt me back to reality.

Scratch the water. I needed something with sugar.

I wandered down the candy isle and when I spied a pack of SweeTarts, bile rose in my throat. Once my favorite candy, it now ignited my gag reflex.

Lovely.

Avoiding all the food, I went toward the back and the row of drink coolers. I stood there staring at all the choices for long minutes without processing what I was seeing. Finally, I blinked and opened the glass door and reached in for a Sprite.

I felt sort of numb. I guess I was in shock. It wasn't every day a girl had a gun pointed at her face. Not even Craig had done that to me.

I let the door slip from my grasp and it fell shut with a thud. An image reflected in the glass in front of me.

There was a man standing right behind me.

He was menacing and intimidating. Waves of anger rolled off him.

I spun around, startled.

Craig curled his upper lip at me and practically snarled.

"How did you know I was here?" I gasped and held the bottle of soda between us like it was a weapon.

"What the fuck are you doing in his car?" he asked, stepping toward me.

I took a step back, trying to recover the distance between us. My back came up against the cooler door, the chilly temp of the glass shocking me through my shirt.

"I'm having car trouble," I said, hating that I was explaining. But I was scared. I knew I shouldn't be, but I was.

Craig's eyes raked over my body and fastened on my shirt. Adam's shirt.

"Are you wearing his clothes?" he rumbled low, but it might well have been a roar.

Yes. Yes, I was. And it reminded me that I wasn't with Craig anymore. It was over. He didn't own me. I pushed off the cooler and moved to walk past him.

He grabbed me by the arm and tossed me back to hit the glass again.

I glanced around for someone that had seen, someone I could signal for help. No one was there.

"I'm leaving," I said in a strong, even voice.

"You can leave when I say you can," he replied.

Men like him were so incredibly arrogant. He thought he could walk into any place, even a public place, and dominate me. He thought he could get away with it. In a way, I guess he was. Craig knew how to abuse me in the most quiet of ways. He knew exactly how far he could push without drawing anyone's eye.

"I'm just here to remind you about our appointment tomorrow morning."

"I told you I'm not coming."

His hands fisted at his sides and he leaned in close. I didn't flinch or cower away. "Listen here, you little whore," he whispered. The scent of cinnamon schnapps on his breath made me gag. I couldn't force it back, and my shoulders heaved.

Craig grabbed my chin, crushing it in his grip and pinning my head against the cooler door. "You might be spreading your legs for Mr. Playboy. Maybe he's even filling your head with pretty lies," he said. "But you're mine. And you *will* do this."

I jerked my head out of his grasp and shoved him away from me. He bumped into the rack behind him and chip bags fell to the floor. His eyes widened in shock that I would dare put my hands on him.

"Don't ever touch me again," I said. I rushed past him and up to the counter. I dug some money out of the bottom of my bag and slapped it on the counter. "Pump three," I told the cashier as she reached for the cash.

"And this," I said, holding up the soda. "Keep the change."

I rushed out of the mart as fast as I could go.

With shaking hands, I fumbled with my bag, trying to find the keys. When I pulled them out, they fell from my grasp onto the pavement. I bent to pick them up and noted a pair of dirty sneakers stepping up beside me.

His knuckles slammed into my side, and I made a high-pitched sound. I stumbled over and caught myself from falling with my palm.

Pain radiated through my middle and scorched across my lower back. Craig grabbed a fistful of my hair and yanked my head to the side so he could whisper-yell in my ear. I felt the disgusting spray of spittle slap against my ear as he spoke. "Be there tomorrow or that punch will be the very least of the ways I'll make you suffer."

He shoved me down and stalked away.

I climbed in the BMW and locked the doors.

Once Craig had driven away, in the opposite direction I needed to go, I drove home in silence. I barely noticed the pain in my side because the aching in my chest was much worse.

I had a really bad feeling about this.

Just as I thought, Harlow was at our place. She was in the bathroom curling her hair when I hurried past on my way to my room.

"Hey, stranger!" she called out.

"Hey, yourself!" I called back, trying to inject some kind of enthusiasm in my tone. I went into my room as my chin wobbled.

I would not cry. *I would not.*

I distracted myself by pulling out an oversized duffle bag and throwing in a bunch of stuff. I didn't need all this crap for one night at Adam's, but I figured this way I didn't have to think and could match something up later, so I just kept shoving it in.

When I was done, I pulled out a pair of dark skinny jeans, wedge heels, and a pink top with a draping cowl neck.

Just as I was about to change, Harlow appeared in my doorway. "Everything okay?" she asked.

"Yeah," I answered. "Just changing for work."

"So you're the boss now, huh?" she said.

I laughed. "Guess so."

"And you and Adam…" She trailed off, her eyes wide and her smile cheeky.

"Adam's amazing," I said, fingering the shirt I was still wearing.

Harlow bounced farther into the room and threw her arms around me. "I'm so happy for you guys!"

"Thanks," I said, returning the hug. I didn't realize how much I needed one.

"You two are perfect together," she said, pulling back.

I wasn't sure I was perfect with anyone, but I didn't burst her bubble. "Hey, I'm going to be staying at Adam's tonight."

She wagged her eyebrows at me. "Is he a good kisser?" she asked.

"Duh," I said.

We both laughed and some of my tension relaxed.

"I knew it," Harlow sang and walked toward the door.

"Hey," I said, and she turned back.

"You should stay at Cam's tonight."

Her brows drew together. "We were going to stay here tonight."

I shook my head. "Stay at Cam's."

I didn't want her anywhere near this place. I was afraid of what Craig might do. He was very angry, and if he came here looking for me…

"Roxie, what's going on?"

"He's been coming around," I admitted. "He's said the most awful things." I couldn't stop the broken sob ripping out of my throat. "Threats."

"He's threatened you?" Harlow asked sharply.

I only nodded. "He was drunk." I made an excuse. "He'll probably forget all about it when he sobers up."

That was a lie. Craig never forgot anything.

"Maybe we should call the police."

Maybe we should have. I'd protected Craig for far too long. In a way, it had only made him worse. In trying to help him, I'd become his enabler.

It was the worst feeling I'd had in a long time.

I had only wanted to love him.

"I don't know what to do," I whispered.

Harlow hugged me again. The silence of the room was interrupted by my cell going off. Harlow stepped back, and I pulled it out of my bag.

It was Adam.

"Hey," I said.

"Get your ass to work," he said gruffly into my ear. Then in a much softer tone, he followed up his order with, "I miss you."

"Me too," I echoed. A feeling of homesickness washed over me. The sound of his voice made me want to see him. To touch him.

"I love you, sweetheart," he said, and then he hung up.

His words made me hurt a little bit less.

"Adam?" Harlow asked, a smile on her lips.

I nodded.

"Talk to him, Roxie. Let him help you deal with Craig."

I agreed, but only because I didn't know what else to say. I didn't want Adam and Craig anywhere near each other.

"So you'll stay at Cam's tonight?" I asked before taking my clothes in the bathroom to do my makeup and hair.

"Sure." She conceded. "Call me tomorrow?"

"Of course!" I said, relieved.

Harlow went into her room to finish getting ready for work, and I took all my stuff in the bathroom. "See ya at work!" I called before shutting myself inside and hunching over the sink.

A flashback of the gun being pointed at me earlier made me squeeze my eyes shut.

Be there tomorrow or that punch will be the very least of the ways I'll make you suffer.

My head snapped back. I stared at myself in the mirror, truth reflecting back from my tired eyes. The only way Craig could truly make me suffer is by hurting those I cared most about. By hurting Adam.

That gun wasn't meant for me. It was meant for him.

I made it to the toilet in time to throw up. After my stomach was completely empty, I rested my cheek on the cold porcelain of the seat.

What the hell was I going to do?

28

Adam

I looked up and smiled as someone stepped into the office, expecting it to be Roxie.

But it was Harlow.

"Hey," I said, letting my smile slip away.

"Can we talk?" she said, keeping her voice low.

I motioned for her to take a seat. She bypassed it and stood just on the other side of my desk.

"What's going on with Roxie?"

I frowned. "What do you mean?"

"I mean she's jumpy as hell, shaking, and made me promise to stay at Cam's tonight. She didn't want us at our place."

"Where is she?" I asked, grim.

"She'll be here any minute. We left at the same time."

I nodded. "I'll talk to her."

"She told me Craig threatened her," Harlow burst out.

I jumped out of my chair. "When?" I growled. I'd had just about enough out of Craig. If I didn't know a loser like him couldn't afford that red car following me around today, I would have thought it was him.

"I don't know," she answered, stepping back.

"Thanks for telling me," I said, trying to keep the anger from my tone.

"You won't leave her alone tonight, right?" Harlow asked.

I couldn't be mad because she was only looking out for Roxie. "No. She'll be safe. I promise."

Harlow looked like a ten-pound weight lifted off her shoulders. "Thanks, Adam."

Roxie passed Harlow on her way out. "What was that about?" she asked, her eyes narrowing.

"Work shit." I lied. I didn't even feel bad about it. I'd lie a million times over if I thought it would protect her.

Roxie nodded and gave me a small smile. "Hi."

I came around the desk, taking in her tight jeans and heels. Her hair was pulled up on the top of her head, and I could tell she spent some time on her face. But all the makeup in the world couldn't cover the tension lines beside her eyes.

I reached around and shoved the door shut and pulled her into my arms. She melted against me like ice cream on a hot summer sidewalk. I knew by the way she curled her fingers into my back that something happened.

A sharp knock on the door broke the moment and Roxie jumped. I tightened my arms around her and held her close. "Yeah?" I called over her head.

"Delivery guy's here. Needs a check and a signature," Cam yelled.

"I'll be right there! Hey, so good news," I told her.

"What is it?" she asked, tilting her head back to peer up at me.

"Stock got delayed and the guys at the club finished their shit early, so I'm staying here tonight, with you." The stock was delayed, but last I spoke to the foreman over at Hatter II, the crew was still there working.

Like I said; I'd lie if I thought it would protect her.

"You are?" she asked. The relief in her violet eyes tempted me to drag her out of this place and home with me that instant.

"Yep. Think you can handle an entire night of training?"

She smiled. It was a welcome sight. "Sure."

"Sweet." I kissed her quickly and then pulled away. "I gotta go out front."

I decided not to mention the fact that someone was following me around today, any of the things Harlow said, or the fact that it was clear something was off.

We had work to do, and this wasn't the place to get into it. I'd ask her later at my place.

But until then, I was sticking close.

It was just a normal night at the club. Drinks, men, music, and half-naked women. We were busy, but that wasn't really anything out of the ordinary. Myrtle Beach did have a slow season, and I guess the club felt it a little, but it didn't come until much later in the year. Usually business was steady even in the fall because the locals came and people drove in.

I made sure to go around and talk to everyone, a lot of the regulars and even some of the newer faces. I didn't do it often, but I did it enough so people knew my face and that I owned the club. It wasn't a secret Mad Hatter II was opening soon, and I was looking for another manager. I'd had a couple guys ask for the job.

Thing was I thought a woman would be better at running the place.

Not all men were like me; not all the club owners around here treated his dancers the way he should. At least if I hired a woman, I would know the girls in this club would be treated the way they should.

'Course, not all women were cut out for the job either.

But Roxy was.

She was a natural.

I walked around, introducing her as the new manager of the place, and I made it clear she was the one who would be calling the shots. I'd known Roxie was popular. Hell, she was the best dancer I had. But I hadn't realized just how liked she was.

She had a smile for everyone. A laugh. An inside joke.

It made me wish I were introducing her as my girlfriend and not my employee.

I thought about just slipping it into a conversation and waiting to see how she'd react, but I wasn't going to manipulate her that way. When I introduced her as mine, I was going to make sure it was exactly what she wanted.

Some of the men were skeptical; they made some comments about taking orders from a woman. I went back to those tables once Roxie had moved on and let them know what I thought of their disrespect. I also made sure Ty, the head bouncer, knew their faces because these guys had one shot or they were out.

Once you got thrown out of my club, you didn't get back in. Period.

After all the socializing was done, I retreated to my office to make some calls and check in with the foreman at Hatter II. I left Roxie to run the floor and take care of the place. After I cleared off all the paperwork I had waiting, I remembered a couple forms I wanted to go over with her, so I went to the corner of the office and crouched down to the bottom drawer of the file cabinet.

Seconds later, Roxie pulled open the door and strode in. The door shut definitively behind her and she leaned against it and took a deep breath.

"What's wrong?" I asked, straightening up and stepping out of the corner.

She jerked in surprise and put a hand up to her chest. "Crap!" she said. "I didn't see you there. You scared the shit out of me."

"Why do you look like you came in here to hide?" I pressed.

"I guess I just need a break from the crowd."

"Try again," I told her.

She sighed. "There's a guy out there who gives me the creeps."

"Show me," I said, moving toward the door, but she blocked me from opening it.

"It's probably nothing."

"If it was nothing, you wouldn't be hiding."

"I'm just jumpy lately," she mumbled.

"Yeah. We'll talk about that later," I intoned. She eyed me out of the corner of her eye but didn't say anything. "So what's with the guy? He say something to you?"

She shook her head. "No. It's just this… feeling I get. You know?"

I nodded.

"I've seen him in here before, in the past couple of weeks. I just… I don't like the way he looks at me."

I lifted her and moved her away. She made a frustrated sound as I pulled open the door. "Show me," I said.

She edged herself in front of me to peak around the door and then popped back inside. "Against the wall. He has a hat on. Sitting alone with a beer and his cell in his hand."

I picked him out in two seconds flat. Our eyes connected. I got a bad feeling.

I didn't like him either.

"He's been in here before?" I asked.

She nodded.

"And you never said anything?"

She shrugged.

"You know the way I do things," I scolded her. Any of the girls that worked here could come to me at any time if there was a guy in here bothering her or making her uncomfortable. I didn't tolerate it. And it wasn't just because this was Roxie. It was *all* the girls in here.

If they got a bad feeling, it was usually because the dude was up to no good, and I had no problem telling them to leave. I'd done it on more than one occasion. I'd never had to do it on Roxie's request, though.

And yeah, maybe since it was her, I felt a little more violent toward this guy, but it still didn't change how I ran my business.

"I feel stupid," Roxie said.

"Listening to your gut is never stupid," I said and motioned for Ty with my chin. I left her in the doorway and stalked over to the guy's table. Ty joined me, standing at my side.

The guy wearing a hat looked up.

"What's up, man?" I said, giving him a gesture with my chin.

"Chillin'," he said, laying down his phone. Face down.

"Time to go," I told him.

"You can't kick me outta here," he said, picking up his beer like he was just getting comfortable.

I plucked the brew right out of his hand. "I just did," I growled.

A muscle in his jaw ticked. I stared him down calmly.

"On what grounds?" he said, sitting up.

"On the grounds that I don't like you." I crossed my arms over my chest and stepped back for him to leave.

"This is bullshit." He picked up his phone and stood, knocking the chair over in the process.

"There's plenty of other clubs," I said.

"Yeah, well, maybe I like the view in this one." His eyes flicked across the room. I followed his gaze to Roxie, who was standing at the bar, loading drinks onto a tray for Harlow.

The urge to knock out all of his teeth was so strong I actually flinched. Ty laid a hand on my shoulder. "I got this, boss," he said and grabbed the asshole by the arm. "Let's go."

Ty led him to the door, and he strolled like he was at the fucking park.

When Ty shoved him out, the guy turned and looked at Roxie one last time.

He winked as the door swung closed.

I gave Ty the signal he wasn't allowed back in this place. It didn't make me feel any better, and I considered rushing out in the parking lot and kicking his ass.

I glanced at Roxie. She'd gone pale.

All the piss and vinegar I felt drained away.

I stalked over and waited until she finished what she was doing. Then I took her hand and led her into the office and shut the door.

"I wanna show you something," I said.

"Okay." She followed me farther into the room.

I led her behind the desk and pulled open the bottom drawer on the left. I lifted up a pile of folders and revealed a black pistol. "I always keep this in here. It's loaded. The safety is off. And yeah, I have a permit."

I glanced up at her. She was staring at the gun with wide eyes.

Fuck. Maybe putting a woman in charge of this kind of place was a shitty idea. I'd rather have some pig running the place than worrying about her every night here alone.

But she wouldn't be alone. There was an entire staff of bouncers, and now she knew where the gun was.

"Rox," I said, making sure she was listening.

"Hmm?" she said, still staring at the gun.

"All you gotta do is point and pull the trigger."

"Okay."

"Have you ever shot a gun before, sweetheart?"

Her eyes pulled away from the weapon to me. "No."

I was booking us time at the range ASAP. She needed to learn. I couldn't always be with her and at least this way I knew she had some protection.

"Just point and shoot," I repeated.

"I think I can handle that," she said, giving me a smile.

I found myself praying I hoped we never had to find out.

29

Roxie

Time at the club passed slowly. It seemed like the night dragged on forever. It didn't help that I analyzed every new and unfamiliar face I saw. I'd become so suspicious of everyone.

The more I thought about it, the more I knew Craig was the one who sent someone after Adam. It was sheer luck that I was in that car instead. Craig didn't respect me, he didn't value me, but I knew he wouldn't kill me.

At least not until I did the stupid porn and made him the money he wanted.

But since it wasn't Craig in that car with the gun, that meant I didn't know who it had been. Craig knew a lot of people, and he only brought a handful of them around. The rest of the people he saw when he was out, which was practically all the time.

So every person in this place was a potential harbinger of doom.

Harbinger of doom = someone who wanted to hurt Adam (or worse).

And yeah, the man I'd been seeing in here every so often, he wasn't exactly an unfamiliar face, but he truly creeped me out. I just couldn't take it tonight. I was relieved when Adam threw him out, but the way he looked at me as the door was swinging closed…

I shuddered.

"Hey," Adam said, coming up behind me. "You cold?"

"Uh, yeah." I lied. I wasn't cold; I was scared.

He chuckled, the warm, rich sound sliding over me like silk. "There you go claiming more of my clothes." Adam slipped a jacket over my shoulders, a navy blue one. I pulled it around me and inhaled his scent.

"Let me just lock up the back and then we can go," he said, jingling a set of keys in his palm.

"Shouldn't I do that?" I asked. "Technically, it's my job."

"Don't tell the boss what a slacker you are." He winked and went to lock up.

I smiled, but it soon faded. What if something happened to him?

I wouldn't be able to live with myself. I wouldn't be able to live without him.

Okay. Yes. I could technically live without him, but my life sure as hell wouldn't be any good. My stomach tightened and I felt a tingling sensation in the back of my throat, like I was going to vomit. I went around the bar and grabbed a bottled water out of the cooler.

The wet, textured hard plastic top did not want to unseal. I tried and then tried again. My palm and fingers turned red from the cap digging into my skin, yet the water was still unopened.

I set it down on the bar top with a thud and dropped my head in my hand.

Adam showed me his gun earlier. How the hell was I supposed to use a gun when I couldn't even open a water?

A laugh bubbled out of me, but it sounded more like a sob.

I heard the crack of the seal on the water and looked up. Adam set the bottle in front of me with no cap. I didn't say anything as I picked up the drink and let the cool water flow down my throat. It felt good going down, almost like it froze some of the emotion going haywire inside of me.

"C'mon, let's go." Adam waited until I came around and he took my hand. On the way out, he set the alarm code and locked the door behind us.

We walked silently across the parking lot toward the BMW. My footsteps stalled. "Where's my car?" I asked, searching everywhere for it.

"I dropped it off to get fixed."

I swung around with wide eyes. "You did?"

"Of course." He said it like it was a given.

I suppose I should have thought it was after what he said to me earlier when he gave me the Roadster to drive. But hearing it and living it were two different things.

"Thank you," I said sincerely. "I'll cover the bill—" I began, but he cut me off.

"There is no bill."

My mouth formed a little O.

"Those jackasses are fixing what they screwed up and you aren't paying for shit. They are."

I didn't know what to say. I was impressed and beyond touched he did this.

"I'll drive," he said and held his hand out for the keys.

I handed them over, and he opened the passenger-side door for me to get in. He didn't just close the door, though. Instead, he leaned inside, his large frame taking up a lot of the space, and pulled the seatbelt around me. It clicked into place, but his fingers lingered, caressing me.

"Long night, huh?"

"You have no idea," I murmured, intoxicated by him.

The entire drive to his place, I kept my eye on the rearview mirror for anyone who might be following us. I peered at the drivers in the cars beside us, and I gripped my hands together in my lap because I was nervous. When the security gates of his community closed behind the car, I sighed with relief.

He carried my bag up to the condo, and I tried to force out all the anxiety in my chest and listened instead to the sound of the nearby crashing waves.

Inside, the condo was dark, but the minute we entered, Adam flipped on several lights and dropped my stuff by the door. I kicked off my heels and padded directly across the open-concept room toward the large windows with the sweeping view. The moon was high above the water, and the inky sky glittered with stars.

I couldn't see much of the ocean other than the constant white-capped waves crashing against the sand.

Adam's arms encircled me from behind and he balanced his chin on my shoulder. "I think we need to talk."

God, I dreaded those words.

As if everything I told him last night about my past wasn't bad enough, now I had to tell him about the man with the gun, the porn, and all of Craig's threats. I wish I didn't have to, but he was involved now. He needed to know to be extra cautious.

Hell, what if being cautious wasn't enough?

"We should go away." My voice was wistful. "Just get out of here for a while."

Adam nuzzled the side of my neck and I tilted my head to the side to give him greater access. "Spending time holed up in a hotel room or a nice resort with you sounds amazing, but I can't help but think you have an ulterior motive besides just wanting to be alone with me."

I covered his forearm with my hand, gripping his solid muscular arm.

"Harlow's worried about you," he murmured.

"On my way home earlier today, I was followed by a strange car. When I pulled off the road, it sped up and the driver pulled out a gun." The words rushed out of me in one great whoosh.

The silence that followed was deafening.

"Someone shot at you today?" Adam finally said. His words were bone-chillingly calm and quiet.

"No. They had the gun out. They pointed at me, but then they drove away."

Adam pulled away and paced around behind me. I didn't need to turn and look to know he was agitated and pissed.

"Did you get plate numbers? A description of the driver?" he demanded.

My shoulders slumped. "No. It happened so fast and then he sped away."

"It was a man?" His voice sharpened.

"I'm pretty sure," I said. Then because I knew he would ask, I added, "It wasn't Craig."

"What kind of car does he drive?" Adam asked, surprising me.

"Some red sports car-looking thing," I replied.

"Son of a bitch," Adam growled. "How the fuck does he pay for that car?"

I turned and faced him. "What?"

"He was following me around today. He drove off when I got out to confront him."

I wasn't surprised and I nodded grimly. "He's been doing that a lot."

"Harlow said he threatened you."

Gee, thanks, Harlow, I thought. But I guess I understood because if I were worried about her, I'd go straight to Cam.

"He owes money to some people. It's how he paid for that car and who knows what else?" I explained. "He wants me to help him repay his debt."

"You're not a fucking ATM!" Adam roared and punched the air.

Without thinking about it, I shrank back against the glass. I hated myself for doing that. I knew, *knew* Adam wouldn't hurt me. But I couldn't stop the almost reflex of reacting that way when a man started yelling and throwing his arm around.

Unfortunately, even in his anger, Adam noted my reaction.

It made me feel ashamed.

"Aww, Rox." All the anger drained away and his voice quieted to almost a whisper. "I didn't mean to yell, sweetheart."

"I know," I said, still watching him through wary eyes.

"I swear to God I would cut off my arm before I ever hurt you."

"I know," I said again.

He cursed beneath his breath.

He took a tentative step toward me. When I didn't try to stop him, he took another. "I'm sorry," he murmured, reaching out. I put my hand in his.

Gently, he tugged me away from the window and into the solid wall of his chest. His palm came up to cup the back of my head, and I closed my eyes.

"I hate that guy," he said, making my chest tighten. "I can't stand the things he's done to you."

That made two of us.

"Why didn't you tell me?" he asked.

"What good would it have done?" I replied. "I thought he would get tired of following me around and stop."

"But he hasn't."

"No," I said, my voice cracking. "And now I've dragged you into this mess. *My* mess."

"You can't drag a man who was already running in your direction," he drawled.

I squeezed my eyes closed. "That man wasn't after me today, Adam. I was in your car. Once he saw it was me behind the wheel, he left."

"Some lowlife with a gun doesn't scare me."

"Oh, I didn't know you were bulletproof," I said, pulling back to look at him. This wasn't a joke. I needed to make him understand that.

"Nothing is going to happen to me," he vowed.

Emotion rose up within me, causing tears to form in my eyes. "If I had stayed with him, you wouldn't be in danger."

Adam gripped me by the shoulders. "Don't ever say that again. I'd take ten bullets. Hell, I'd die before I let you go back to him."

"I don't want you to die," I whispered.

"I'm not going anywhere. I have too much to live for." He stroked my cheek.

"Make love to me." I was tired of talking. Tired of being scared. I wanted to feel something more. I wanted to feel him.

Adam swept me up into his arms and carried me into the dark bedroom. He didn't bother with the lights, but it was okay because we didn't need to see. Everything we did was done by touch.

And for a little while, I forgot everything outside of this room.

But I knew, deep down, when the sun came up, there would be no forgetting.

30

Adam

The higher the sun rose in the sky, the more I began to realize we should have spent more time talking last night and less in bed.

But when she looked up at me with tear-filled violet eyes and asked me to make love to her, I was fucking lost. There was no way in hell I could deny her anything.

Watching her flinch away with my outburst was probably one of the worst feelings I'd ever had. And that's saying a lot considering the number of wives I've had. I never wanted to be someone she ever had to think twice about. I never wanted her to wonder about her safety or my intentions toward her.

Of course, she had yet to actually tell me she was mine. She'd yet to tell me she loved me, even though I whispered it to her all night long.

We were still lying in bed, the sheets tangled around our legs as I lightly drew my fingers up and down her back. She wasn't a morning person; I'd known this about her for a long time. But I knew she was awake. I knew her brain was working overtime, and I felt the tension in her limbs.

"There's a present in the kitchen for you," I said.

Her head popped up and she gazed down at me in surprise. "What kind of present?"

"You'll have to go look and see." The excitement in her eyes and the way they twinkled made me wish I'd bought her something more.

For not being a morning person, she sure bounded out of the bed awfully fast. One of my T-shirts was draped across the dresser and she snagged it on her way out the door and pulled it over her head.

Amused, I followed her into the kitchen where her present was sitting with a big red bow on the top. Roxie saw it and squealed, running over to the box like it was a bag of money.

"I've always wanted one of these!" she exclaimed, literally hugging the box to her chest. She pulled the bow off the top and stuck it to the counter and began ripping open the box.

I laughed and stepped forward to help her. "You're torturing the box."

"Nothing stands between a girl and her coffee," she quipped.

I shook my head, loving the fact that whatever seemed to be weighing on her in bed wasn't as important as this Keurig.

"Do you know how to work this thing?" I asked as I slid the large black machine out and onto the counter.

She looked at me like I had four heads and began pulling off all the wrapping and prepping it to make coffee. She sure worked like she knew what she was doing, so I stood back and enjoyed the show.

In no time, she commandeered a spot on the counter, plugged it in, and had the water reservoir filled with filtered water from the fridge. She was so happy with this simple gift that it made me love her more.

Christmas this year was going to be fucking epic.

Suddenly, she gasped and spun around. "I need K-cups!" she went back to the box and started sifting through the packaging.

I laughed and opened up a nearby cupboard. She didn't even pay attention. I cleared my throat and she glanced up. A smile broke out over her face as she studied the several boxes of K-cups I'd stocked up on. "I didn't know what kind so I just got a bunch."

She leapt at me, throwing herself into my arms and planting kisses over my face. Before I could turn it into a steamy make-out session, she was gone again, and the rich scent of coffee filled the kitchen.

She filled two mugs expertly and reached for the fridge. "Please tell me you have milk."

I snagged the coffee closest to me off the counter and sipped the black brew while hiding a smile. She gasped again when she saw the neat row of creamer filling the top shelf.

"I didn't know what kind you liked…" I began, but she finished for me.

"So you just got a bunch."

I nodded, but she wasn't paying attention to me. She went for the mocha creamer, and I made a note in my brain that was probably her favorite. After she added a generous amount to the cup, she leaned against the counter, cupped the steaming mug in both hands, and took a sip.

Her eyes slid closed and she moaned in her throat. My cock stirred in my boxers.

"Your coffee maker is better than mine," she said, taking another sip.

"Guess you'll just have to stay here lots."

That didn't elicit the desired effect. In fact, it seemed to drop a dark, rainy cloud over her previously sunny disposition.

"Thank you," she said, ignoring my comment and closing the space between us to lean up and kiss me fully on the lips. When she pulled back, she glanced at the clock.

"Wanna go down on the beach?" I asked her.

I saw the desire in her eyes, but after a second, she shook her head. "Can we stay inside?"

"Coffee in bed?" I asked, arching an eyebrow.

In the bedroom, we opened the curtains so we could stare at the view.

But Roxie didn't seem to notice. She was growing more agitated by the second it seemed.

Antsy.

Yeah, that's how she was behaving. And her eyes kept sliding to the clock.

"Do you need to be somewhere?" I asked, draining what was left of my coffee and setting the mug on the nearby table.

"No," she answered but didn't offer any kind of explanation for her behavior.

A few more minutes of her growing even more distant and I'd had enough. "Rox, what's going on? Is there something you haven't told me?"

"I don't want to tell you," she said.

I knew then it was bad. I tried to steel myself for whatever it was, but how did you prepare for the unknown?

"That probably means you need to tell me right now."

She gave me a look like she had a bad taste in her mouth. A few beats of silence followed, but then she sighed. "Remember how I told you Craig wanted me to help him pay back the money he owes?"

I nodded.

"Well, he kind of had a specific idea on how to make it." Her fingers were turning white around the mug because she gripped it so hard.

"I'm assuming it's a large chunk of money he owes if he's driving that car around," I muttered and scrubbed a hand over my face.

"I'm sure," she replied.

"Sweetheart, you do know you are not responsible for him or the money he owes, right?" It occurred to me while this was blindingly clear to me, maybe she still felt some kind of responsibility toward him.

"I know," she whispered.

"So you told him no?"

She nodded. "Of course I did."

"And that's when he threatened you," I surmised, hating this guy more and more by the second.

Her eyes filled with tears and she set her coffee aside to twist her hands in her lap. When she lifted her jewel-like eyes at me, they were filled with despair. "He threatened you, Adam. He sent someone after you with a gun. He knows I would never do what he wants if it was only my life he was threatening."

A really bad feeling crawled over me. It simmered just below my skin, and my jaw clenched. This guy owed a lot of money, and he wanted Roxie to *do* something to help repay it.

"What does he want you to do, Roxie?" I asked quietly.

"He wants me to be in an adult film." She spoke hesitantly and softly.

She might well have been screaming because just the fucking idea of her screwing some guy on camera for money echoed so loudly through my body that I lost my hearing for several seconds.

I saw her staring at me, saw her lips form my name.

But I didn't hear.

I'd never in my entire life had the urge to kill someone like I did right then. Sure, I threatened to kill him in my head several times, but this… this time I had to physically stop myself from leaving the house and hunting him down.

I felt Roxie's hand on my forearm and I glanced down. Reality came rushing back, and I realized I wasn't on the bed anymore. I wasn't even in the bedroom. I was standing in the living room with my car keys in my palm.

"Adam," she pleaded, "where are you going?"

"Nowhere," I said, forcing the words past my lips. After a moment, I tossed the keys on the couch and sat down on the coffee table.

Not only was that motherfucker trying to pimp Roxie out, but he was using me to do it. Part of me realized it said a lot about how Roxie felt about me if even her ex realized a threat to me would make her do what he wanted. But I couldn't think about that now.

"You aren't considering this," I said, hoarse.

"I told you I said no." She sat on the couch across from me. "I'm supposed to meet him today, this morning, at some address he gave me."

"Give me the address," I said hard.

"No."

I glanced up. "I'm not kidding."

"I'm not either." Her jaw was set and her eyes were stone. "I'm not going and neither are you."

"You want me to just let him get away with this?"

"I want you to just get away with me," she whispered. "You already won, Adam. You have what he doesn't. Me."

"Ah, sweetheart, having you isn't a contest. You aren't some pawn I can use to stick it to him. I love you."

"And I'm with you now."

It was the first time she really confirmed it. My heart skipped a beat. "You making it official?" I asked, the corner of my lip tilting up.

She nodded. "But promise me you'll stay away from him."

I felt my lips thin. How the hell was I supposed to promise that?

"I mean it, Adam. I'm tired of him. I just want out. I want away from it all. I just want to be with you and not look over my shoulder. Don't let my past get in the way of our future."

"I'll stay away from him," I swore, taking her hand. "But if he comes at me, I'm not making any promises."

"I wouldn't expect you to." Roxie sank her teeth into her bottom lip, looking worried. "I won't show up today, and he'll realize he can't control me anymore. He'll leave us alone then."

I switched onto the couch and pulled her into my arms, resting my chin on top of her head.

I wondered if she really believed he was just going to go away.

I didn't think it was going to be that easy.

31

Roxie

It had been a week since I didn't show up to the address Craig gave me, and I had yet to see or hear from him.

Part of me was shocked he'd given up so easily, and another part of me was just so incredibly relieved. I hoped he would give up. I thought he might, but deep down I was still terribly afraid he wouldn't.

Adam hadn't seen him either. There had been no suspicious cars following us, no gun-waving strangers… no threats of any kind. Still, we were both cautious and watchful on a daily basis. When we weren't at work, we spent a lot of time at his place. The gated property made me feel safe.

Honoring my wishes, Harlow was staying at Cam's. I missed our time together, the time we just hung out in the living room for girl talk, but I knew we'd have it again. Right now, being safe was the thing to do.

I will admit after a week of nothing, I was starting to relax and feel better about things. Adam and I settled into a routine of sorts, but it wasn't the kind of routine that made a person wake up in the morning and think "just another day." No, this was the kind of routine—a kind of life—I prayed would last the rest of my life.

I woke up every morning in his arms and went for a run on the beach with him. Well, he ran and I gasped for breath and stumbled around. He said I'd get better with time. I really didn't care. I liked the view from behind him.

Then we would shower. Long, lazy showers that always involved more than soap. We'd have coffee together and I'd make breakfast (Adam was a complete disaster in the kitchen), and we'd eat it on the small balcony and watch the waves. Of course, the majority of our days were spent at work. Adam was over at the Mad Hatter II and I was at the original club. Turns out I liked being a manager. And I didn't miss dancing at all.

Sometimes we'd get away for dinner or lunch, and every single night I spent wrapped up in his arms.

I could honestly say I'd never been happier in my entire life.

He was everything I ever wanted, but over the years I thought that was only a dream. It blew my mind the stark differences being with him compared to being with my ex.

Of course, I knew time would be the real test. My relationship with Adam was just getting started, and I'd learned from bitter experience that things were always good in the beginning. Keeping what we had was going to be the hard part.

I'd be a liar if I didn't admit Adam's past marriages made me nervous. Holding on to a relationship seemed hard for him. Both of us had histories to leave behind, and more than anything, I wanted a future with him.

I loved him.

I truly wondered if I would ever again be able to let someone in enough to love them. Yes, I've always had a soft spot for Adam, and maybe it was our long-standing friendship and work relationship that made it easier to take the plunge. It made it easier to admit to myself.

How could I *not* love him?

I still hadn't told him. He never pushed. He never held back his own declaration of love. He just simply accepted me, simply loved me.

I'd never been loved like this before.

A secret smile played on my lips as I walked through the parking lot toward my Mazda. The air-conditioning worked better than ever, and it had new tires to boot.

There was a cool breeze pulling through my straight hair today, the kind that reminded me it actually was fall. I loved days like these, such a welcome break from the heat.

I was going to have to swing by my place later and get my boots. It was great weather for them with a pair of jeans. I climbed into the car, adjusting the loose top I was wearing over my low-cut jeans. The sting of pain was constant, but I ignored it.

Adam was at work, and he thought I was too, so I pointed the car in the direction of the Mad Hatter. I had some paperwork and an order for some liquor to put in before we opened tonight. Harlow and Cam were both working tonight, and I wondered what Harlow would say when I told her where I was this afternoon.

The inside of the club was quiet and still, but it didn't scare me. Adam told me about the restraining order and how Craig wasn't allowed even in the parking lot. Of course, the restraining order I filed a week ago (at Adam's insistence) to keep Craig away from me pretty much protected me everywhere I went.

But here at the club, I felt double protected.

I turned on the lights out in the bar and grabbed a water from the cooler before heading into the office. I laid my cell phone on the corner of the desk and started pulling out paperwork and the order form for the supplier.

I considered turning on the radio but decided to enjoy the quiet before the club opened and the place was filled with noise.

The silence was disrupted by the sound of the main entrance banging shut. I sat up a little straighter, staring out the office door but unable to see who it was. A smile broke over my face because I knew it was probably Adam.

I couldn't wait to show him my surprise.

I left the desk and rushed out of the office. I made it two steps into the main room before I halted in shock.

It wasn't Adam.

It was Craig.

And he wasn't alone.

He looked horrible, the worst I'd ever seen him. His dark hair was greasy and unwashed, standing up around his head in great clumpy spikes. His T-shirt and jeans were dirty, ripped, and hung off his thinner frame. But what was most concerning was the state of his face.

It was battered and beaten.

Clearly, he'd been injured badly. Both eyes were blackened, one was slightly puffy, and there was an angry welt slashing through one of his eyebrows. His lips were cracked and dried. He had a huge yellowing bruise on his jaw. His nose was swollen and crooked like it was broken. Actually, he had a lot of ugly yellowing bruises on his face. I wondered what the rest of his body looked like under his clothes.

"You can't be here," I told him. "I have a restraining order."

"First I've heard of it," he said, giving me a squinty angry look.

"Leave."

"Did you think I'd just accept the fact you didn't show?" he said, stepping forward. The other two men hung in the background.

"The bouncer is going to be here any minute." I lied. Maybe if he knew someone was on their way, he'd get out while he could.

"No, he isn't." Craig snarled. "I've been watching you, you stupid bitch. You've been shacking up all week with that guy who owns the place. I always knew you were screwing him."

I gasped. "I was not." I stayed faithful to him always, even when I shouldn't have.

"We'll see if he still wants you once you're screwing on camera."

I straightened my spine. "I told you. I am *not* doing that movie." I wasn't going to have this conversation either. I spun on my heel and went back into the office to get my phone. I was calling the cops. They could haul him in for violating the restraining order.

Craig moved fast, grabbing onto my arm and whipping me around. My knee caught in the chair that sat in front of the desk and it buckled. I didn't fall because Craig yanked me up and dragged me back out into the bar.

"Look at me!" he roared. "All these bruises, the broken bones… you did this to me."

"No," I said, trying to steady myself on my feet.

"These people, they want their money. They want their movie. This…" He gestured toward his battered face. "This was just a warning."

"You shouldn't have made a deal with people like that."

He slapped me. The sharp sound of his hand against my cheek reverberated throughout the room. I let my hair fall over my face and conceal me from view as I composed myself. Then I glanced up and looked at the men who were in the room.

How could they stand by and watch this?

I recognized one of them. It was the man Adam threw out of the bar over a week ago. It was the same guy I'd seen in here before, the one who was always watching me.

Oh my God, did he only come here to spy for Craig?

I glanced at the other man, wondering if I recognized him as well, but I didn't. 'Course, I could barely concentrate on his features when I was so distracted by the large camera in his grip. It had a large spotlight attached to the top of it and looked like it probably weighed about ten pounds.

A sick feeling wormed its way inside me.

"What do you want?" I whispered to Craig.

"I want what you owe me," he growled. "And I'm here to collect."

"No." My voice wavered.

He motioned for the guy with the camera, and the man hoisted it up on his shoulder, and the blinding spotlight clicked on and shined in my eyes.

"What better place to film an adult film that on the stage of a strip club?" Craig mused.

He thought I was just going to perform right here, right now because he slapped me? No way in hell.

I rushed for the office door again and he gave chase, shoving me from behind. I hit the desk and slid across it, scattering most of what was on it onto the floor.

My cell being one of those things.

I scrambled up to lunge for it, but he caught me by the ankle and spun me around, dragging me across the desk. He jumped on me, pinning me to the wooden top, and stared down at me with angry eyes.

Who was this man?

He was so different than the boy I'd met at seventeen.

"You will do this, and when you do, I'll walk away."

"And if I don't?" I asked, struggling against him.

"I'll kill you. And then I'll kill him."

I started to scream. I swung at him, my fist connecting with his jaw, and his head snapped back. I used the momentary distraction to roll out from beneath him. I fell onto the floor, but I kept moving. My phone was just feet away so I scrambled over. Just as my hand closed around it, Craig jabbed his foot into my rib.

The air whooshed out of me, and I sprawled across the floor onto my stomach. The sharp pain in my middle caused me to groan.

"That's it, bitch. Make those sounds in the film."

I sat up and glared at him. "I'll never do it willingly."

He appeared as though a light bulb came on over his head. "Even better."

He grabbed a handful of my hair and dragged me out into the bar. The cameraman trained the camera on us.

"You ready?" he asked the man who used to sit in the bar and stare.

"Oh, I've been ready."

Oh. My. God. Was this the man I was supposed to sleep with in the video? Chunky bile rose up in my throat.

"She's not too willing," Craig said. He made it sound amusing.

The man with the camera smirked. "You know how much money perverts pay for a rape fantasy video? This will pull in a shit ton of money."

They planned to stand here and watch and record this animal raping me and then sell the video for profit?

I'd rather be dead.

I started fighting.

Craig had a hold of my hair so I punched out with my fist and hit him in the side. He made a wheezing sound and released me. I realized I was gripping my phone. I dialed 9-1-1 and hit SEND. Before the operator could answer, the phone was knocked out of my hand and it slid across the floor and under the table.

"Get her," Craig ordered my stalker.

The man I recognized from the bar was wearing jeans and a wife-beater tank top. He gave me a sick grin and stalked forward. I ran to put the nearest table between us. He kept coming.

"You're going to like it," he said. "Fighting me will only make it better."

I gagged and grabbed up a chair that was upside down on the table. I didn't have much arm strength, but I launched the chair over the table at him.

He dodged it easily.

"I like a woman with some spunk," he said, still coming closer.

I started screaming again, yelling for help, and I made my way around the room. I needed to get to my phone, but he was in front of it. Then I remembered the phone behind the bar. I rushed forward, skittering across the floor and behind the bar. My hand closed around the closest bottles of liquor, and I threw them at the man pursuing me.

Craig and the cameraman just stood back and watched like this was the best show they'd ever seen.

A sob ripped from my throat as the man leapt over the wooden bar.

I picked up the phone, but he snatched it out of my hand and dropped it on the ground. His viselike arm went around my waist and lifted me off the ground so my legs were dangling in the air.

He carried me back around the bar, the broken glass crunching beneath his feet. I was kicking and screaming and clawing at his arm. Still he did not let go.

"This one's a little hellcat," he said, directing his words to the camera.

He threw me down on the table and leapt at me, forcing his way between my legs. "No!" I screamed, punching him.

He grabbed my wrists and pinned my arms above my head. With his free hand, he took a handful of my top and yanked, the soft fabric gave way and I heard the seams ripping.

Cool air brushed over my chest as it heaved.

Fat tears rolled across my cheeks as a rough hand gripped my breast and groped it coarsely. He started thrusting his jean-clad hips into me, dry-humping me while I screamed.

He tore away the lace of my bra and snatched my nipple between his finger and thumb and pinched it so hard I cried out.

He grunted and slammed his hips into me. I could see the bulge in his jeans, and it made me sick.

I tried to kick him. I tried to roll away. The more I struggled, the harder he squeezed my breast.

His hand finally released my bruised flesh, but he still pinned my wrists. His free hand reached for the buckle on his jeans.

"Please, no," I whimpered.

"I like a woman who begs." He grunted. He undid his jeans and shoved them down over his hips. He wasn't wearing any underwear, and his penis sprang out and pointed to my body.

I started crying.

I couldn't believe this was happening. I couldn't believe Craig would go so far as to watch me get raped.

My rapist took a moment to stroke his cock, rubbing it back and forth and then dragging it along my clothed core.

I scissored my legs closed and tried to buck him off. He spanked me, leaving my ass burning.

Fight, Roxie, fight!

I could not let them do this to me.

"Drag her to the stage," Craig ordered, his voice cold and lacking emotion. The man kicked off his jeans completely and then pulled me off the table. My knees threatened to buckle, but I held strong. I prepared to kick him, but before I could, he threw me over the table again, stomach side down, and ground his raging hard-on against my ass.

I screamed.

He reached beneath me and I recoiled, his hands on me was the most disgusting thing I'd ever experienced. I felt the buckle on my jeans give way and the zipper slide down. I threw my head back and the crown of my head slammed into his face. He grunted and stumbled back. I rushed away as pieced of my ruined, tattered shirt trailed behind me.

I ran into the office, knowing I could call for help with the landline and then at least barricade myself until the police arrived.

The rush of feet followed along behind me, but I didn't turn to see. I heard Craig ordering the cameraman not to miss a thing, and I heard the grunts of pain from the man who was trying to rape me. I made it inside the office and grabbed the door.

I swung it closed as my attacker charged, blood rushing from his nose.

Like a linebacker, he slammed into the door, bursting it open and splintering the wood. I went flying back and hit my head on the edge of the desk. My body folded and fell onto the floor as pain exploded in my skull.

Rough hands grabbed me. I was thrown onto the desk.

I felt my clothes being ripped off my body and my legs shoved apart.

Inside I was screaming, fighting, and dying of horror. On the outside, I felt fuzzy and sluggish.

"Get her tits again," someone said in the background.

I felt rough hands grab my breasts and pull them away from my body. He was so rough. Not at all the way Adam was.

Adam.

My eyes sprang open and a jolt of clarity came rushing through my head.

"No!" I roared and slid my body across the desk. The rough hands followed me.

I remembered the gun in the bottom of the desk drawer.

I let my arm fall down over the edge of the desk as a set of teeth closed over one of my nipples. I cried out in pain and pulled the drawer open. My hand closed around the gun.

Point and shoot. Adam's words floated through my head with quiet clarity.

I swung up my arm and took aim at the man who was getting ready to spread my legs and rape me.

And then I pulled the trigger.

32

Adam

I called the cops the day after Roxie told me everything. I had a buddy on the force, a guy I'd known for several years, and I told him everything.

Later that day, we went down to the station and I had Roxie fill out papers and make a statement. A protective order was being issued and that scum bucket wouldn't be allowed anywhere near Roxie.

I didn't think he was the type of guy to follow the order, but so far it worked to keep him out of my club so I hoped it might help.

But in reality, that paper was just insurance that when Craig came around, he'd be breaking another law.

A week went by and every night Roxie was in my bed. I'd grown so accustomed to having her there with me I was dreading when she would go back to her own apartment. I thought about asking her to move in permanently, but I knew it was too soon. I had to be smart about this.

I was determined that this relationship was going to last.

I was going to do this right, take things slow. I was going to prove beyond a shadow of a doubt that we were meant to be together and I would never hurt her.

Plus, I figured I should wait until she was able to tell me she loved me before we lived together. It would be years if I ever asked her to marry me, but I'd come to realize that marriage itself didn't matter. It was the commitment between two people. It was the unwavering love that mattered most.

It was kind of liberating to realize that. To know that I'd finally found someone who I didn't have to prove she was the one to myself. I didn't have to get married to convince myself we'd be together forever.

We would be.

I glanced at the clock. There was still over an hour before the Hatter II opened. It was doing well so far. The first couple nights we opened the place had been packed. I was going to work my ass off to make sure it stayed that way.

My cell rang, and I snagged it up, hoping it was Roxie. One glance at the screen told me it wasn't. It was my lawyer.

"This is Adam," I answered.

"Adam, it's Sherman," the man on the other line spoke.

"Sherman," I said, sitting back in my chair and wondering how much this call was going to cost me. Sherman was the best lawyer and well worth the money, but fuck, he was expensive. "What do I owe the pleasure?"

"I don't have very good news, I'm afraid," Sherman spoke.

I sat up a little straighter. "What?"

"I was contacted by the PD a few moments ago. It seems they are having trouble locating Craig Ascott. They have been unable to serve him with the protective order."

Fear spiked in my veins and my heart began thumping a little harder. "What do you mean they can't find him?" I cried. "It's been a goddamned week!"

"Yes, well," Sherman said, clearing his throat. "It seems they've tried contacting him daily and all attempts have turned up empty."

What the fuck was he up to? I knew he wasn't dead. I couldn't be that lucky.

"They said they would keep attempting, but they are beginning to suspect he left town."

I pinched the bridge of my nose. "Thanks for the call, Sherman."

"I'll let you know if and when he is found."

I disconnected the call and slammed the phone on the desk. I didn't like knowing no one knew what he was doing. I thought the cops had this under control.

I thought about Roxie over at the club by herself. She needed to know so she could be extra cautious. I grabbed my keys and phone and jogged out to my car.

As I pulled out of the lot, I called Ty. He picked up on the first ring.

"Hey, boss."

"Ty," I said. I didn't have time for pleasantries. "Can you come in to work early? Roxie's been working there all week before we open. I don't like her being there alone. I'll increase your wages if you can start coming in early to cover security while she's there."

"Sure, boss. Anything for Miss Roxie."

He was as southern as they came. He respected women and he was tough as nails.

"I really appreciate this, Ty."

"I appreciate the raise," he said.

I laughed. "I'll see ya in a bit."

"Yes, sir," he said, and then the line went dead.

Next I punched Roxie's number into my cell. I needed to hear her voice.

Her voicemail picked up on the first ring. I pulled the phone back and looked at it. Then I tried to call her again. Same thing.

The hairs on the back of my neck stood and my foot pressed down on the gas. She was probably just on the line with a supplier or something. She was probably working her ass off, and I was being paranoid.

Still, I didn't slow down.

I broke all the traffic laws on my way to the Mad Hatter. I figured if a cop saw me, he could chase me all the way to the bar. His services might be needed.

But no police officer fell into the path behind me, and I made it to the bar in record time.

As soon as I pulled into the parking lot, I saw a black Honda sitting by the entrance. Beside it was a red car.

Craig's car.

My tires squealed when I slammed the brakes and got out of the car, leaving it running. He was in there with Roxie and they weren't alone.

Adrenaline and sheer fear almost stopped my body from breathing.

And then a gunshot tore through the air.

33

Roxie

The bullet hit my attacker and his body jerked back. I used the moment to scramble up off the desk and stand on shaky legs.

The man I shot stared up at me with wide, shocked eyes as his hand slowly came up to cover the red blooming out across his chest.

I gripped the gun, finger still on the trigger, all too willing to shoot him again.

But it wasn't necessary.

He crumpled to the floor and didn't get back up.

In the doorway, the cameraman stood there in shock, his jaw slack as the bright light on top of the camera shined in my eyes.

I lifted the gun and pointed it at him.

The door to the club slammed open. The sound of the metal hitting against the wall made everyone in the room jump.

"Roxie!" Adam roared. Seconds later, I heard a string of curses and his footsteps crunching over glass.

"I'm here," I said weakly, still pointing the gun at the cameraman.

"What the fuck is going on here?" Adam roared. The camera was pulled off of the man's shoulder and hit the ground with a sharp crack. Adam spun him around by the shoulder, and I heard bones crunch as he plowed his fist into the man's face.

He too crumbled to the floor with his bleeding friend.

Adam looked at me and his face went white. He swayed a little on his feet and stepped over the body of the cameraman. I was still holding out the gun, my arm shaking uncontrollably, and my teeth beginning to chatter.

Adam approached me warily, slowly. "Oh, sweetheart. What happened to you?"

"I shot him," I said, feeling numb.

Adam didn't even glance at the body on the floor. "I'm sure he deserved it."

The desk was still between us when he stopped walking. "Can I have the gun, sweetheart?" he asked, glancing at it pointed toward him.

I knew I didn't need to point it at him, but I just couldn't make myself lower my arm. I nodded as my teeth slammed together, creating a loud clicking noise.

"I'm going to come over there," he said gently and moved around the desk. Slowly, he reached out and peeled the gun from my hand, lowering it to his side.

When the gun was gone, a sob ripped out of my chest.

"Oh, love," he crooned. "Oh shit."

I'd never seen his sun-kissed skin look so pale. His eyes were red-rimmed and the pain on his face was raw. "You're bleeding," he said.

I glanced down at my breast at the blood smeared on my skin. "He bit me," I replied, my voice hollow.

Adam made a strangled sound and began unbuttoning his shirt. He stripped it off quickly and then took a step toward me. "Let's get you covered up," he whispered and pulled it around me.

I pushed my arms through the oversized gray dress shirt as I shook almost uncontrollably. Adam buttoned it up and then glanced at me. "Can I touch you?"

I nodded.

He pulled me into his warm, bare chest. A sob ripped from my throat and they didn't stop. I cried and cried. The sounds leaving my body were almost inhuman. I'd never been so afraid or violated in my entire life.

The man who tried to rape me moaned from the floor.

I jerked and whimpered.

Adam shot him.

He wouldn't be making any more sounds.

I started crying again, and Adam picked me up, cradling me into his chest, and turned to leave the room. The cameraman was sitting against the wall, staring at Adam warily.

"I swear to God," he intoned, "if you so much as move, I will fucking kill you."

I didn't look to see what the man's reaction was, but since I heard nothing at all, I assumed he listened.

Juggling me, the gun, and a cell, Adam dialed 9-1-1. A sound from across the room brought both our heads up.

Craig was up on the stage, having rushed out from behind the curtain where I assumed he was hiding.

He was holding a gun pointed directly at us. "I'm leaving. Don't try and stop me and I won't shoot."

"You fucking piece of lowlife scum," Adam growled. He sounded more animal than man, and it scared me. "The only place you're going is jail. Where little boys like you become toys. I hope you enjoyed whatever the fuck you tried to do here today because worse than that is waiting for you in the slammer."

Craig shouted and leapt off the stage, his shoes making a slapping sound on the floor. I screamed as he raised the gun once more at Adam.

"No!" I screamed as gunfire erupted.

Police sirens cut through the silence that followed the shots.

"Adam!" I screamed, trying to get out of his arms, trying to see where he was shot.

"I'm fine, sweetheart," Adam said, picking up a chair and sitting in it with me in his lap. "He didn't shoot me."

"Then…?" My voice cracked.

"He tried." Adam grunted. "My aim is better."

I tore my eyes from Adam and looked across the room at Craig.

Adam shot him.

I was pretty sure he was dead.

I was sad and relieved all at the same time. I collapsed against Adam's chest. My entire body hurt and I felt so incredibly dirty.

Police rushed through the door, scattering into the room like red ants on a disturbed anthill, all of them with weapons drawn.

"All's clear," Adam called and set the gun down on the floor beside us and lifted his hands where they could see them.

Adam held me while several officers with drawn weapons scurried through the building, looking for more intruders. After several long minutes of searching, they met back in the bar.

"Scene is clear," one of the men said to another man who was stepping through the door.

"Lincoln," Adam said, relief in his voice. "Am I fucking glad to see you."

"When the 9-1-1 call came through with no response and this address, I was afraid I'd find something like this," he said, his eyes focusing on me. I guessed my attempt to call for help had gotten through. Thank God.

"Ma'am." He bobbed his chin toward me.

Lincoln was Adam's friend on the police force. He was at the station when we filled out the protection order paperwork.

I didn't respond. I couldn't. I just buried my face in Adam's neck. His arms tightened around me.

"Looks like we have some casualties," Lincoln surmised. "Get the coroner over here and this place cordoned off."

When men started shuffling around the room, Lincoln spoke to us again. "I'm going to need some statements."

"Can we do it later? She needs medical attention," Adam said.

I lifted my head. "No," I replied. "Let's do it now. The past has haunted me long enough."

Adam pressed a kiss to the side of my head. "You sure, sweetheart?"

"I'm sure," I told him. "Will you stay with me?" I asked.

The question sounded innocent, yet it was anything but. Yes, I wanted him to stay while I recounted the nightmare I'd just endured, but that wasn't all.

I wanted to know if even after all of this, was he still willing to love me?

Adam looked at me like we weren't sitting in the center of a crime scene, like there wasn't a cop waiting to take our statement. He looked at me like I was the only girl in the entire room. His eyes held no disgust for how he found me and the fact there were teeth marks on my breast. He didn't seem to be appalled I'd shot someone.

And I didn't care that he'd literally just killed two men.

"I'm not going anywhere," he murmured, brushing the hair out of my face. "Not ever."

"I love you, Adam," I whispered. "I love you so much."

He sucked in a breath and his chocolate eyes fastened on mine. "You've been through a lot," he murmured, stroking my hair again.

I caught his wrist and gave it a gentle squeeze. "I mean it. I do love you, and I'm never going to stop."

"I love you too, Roxie," he said, and I could see it in his eyes.

"I'm ready," I told Lincoln, who was pretending not to listen to our conversation. He pulled out a pen.

When I was done recounting everything that happened just moments ago, I was exhausted, shaky, and in pain.

But for the first time in a long time, I wasn't scared.

I knew I had a long road of healing ahead, but with Adam by my side, I knew it would be okay.

And my past?

I was finally able to let it go.

EPILOGUE

Adam

I heard her keys in the door all the way into the bedroom. She wasn't really being loud; I was just so in tune with her I couldn't *not* hear her enter the condo.

I stepped out into the living room in time to see her at the kitchen island, dropping her keys and what looked like a bunch of paperwork and some kind of booklet.

Her dark hair was hanging down her back, and the boots that rose to just below her knee totally turned me on.

"Hey," I said, and she looked up.

Her smile was almost blinding when she turned it on me. "Hey."

She crossed the room, and I opened my arms to her and she came into them willingly. "I like your outfit," she said, letting her fingers travel over my lower back to tug at the towel I had wrapped around my waist.

"I just got out of the shower," I said as she pressed against me a little closer.

I closed my eyes and willed my body to keep it cool, but my cock had other ideas. She felt so damn good up against my skin, and the way she was plastering herself against me was totally testing my self-control.

Who was I kidding?

The past couple weeks had been testing my self-control.

It had been almost two months since I made love to Roxie, since before she was assaulted and almost raped at the club. Because of the violence with which she was attacked and the injuries she sustained (broken ribs, bruises, puncture wound due to bite marks, a concussion…), we took sex off the table.

I still wanted her more than ever, but her body and mind needed time to heal. Her bruises were faded, the bite marks on her chest were healed, and the concussion had long since passed. Basically, her physical injuries were mended, but her mind wasn't quite there yet. I think at first she was worried I might be upset if she wasn't ready to have sex, but just having her in my life was enough for me.

She still stayed here most nights, and she always curled into my arms, sometimes our make-out sessions got a little heated, and some days she seemed like she needed more space. I never pushed, but I was always here when she needed me.

She still had nightmares sometimes. They were becoming less and less, but there were still times she would wake up screaming or I'd have to wake her because she was crying.

It made me glad I killed the son of a bitch who tried to rape her and the asshole who set it up.

No charges were pressed against me for shooting and killing Craig and the rapist because it was determined it was all self-defense. Craig shot at me, which gave me the right to shoot back. Plus, he was on property he'd been legally ordered to avoid.

The man I didn't kill, the one with the camera, was currently sitting in jail, charged as an accessory. I hoped he rotted there.

After the investigation, it was strongly suggested that Roxie and I seek counseling for everything we went through. I encouraged Roxie to go, but I didn't go.

The thing was I didn't feel sorry for what I did. Maybe that said something dark about my character, but it wasn't as if I killed two innocent bystanders. One was a rapist. I mean, his dick was literally hanging out when the coroner carted him away. And I had to look at his teeth marks on Roxie's flesh for weeks.

And Craig…

Well, I kept my word to Roxie. I didn't go after him. He came after me, and I finished it. The end.

In my mind, I took two lives, but they were lives that did nothing but create misery. And at least this way, Roxie wouldn't have to look over her shoulder every time she left the house.

I pulled back and looked down at her. "How did registration go?"

"It was good," she said, going over to the window to stare out. "There were a lot of people there and I was nervous, but I did it."

"Yeah?"

She looked over her shoulder and gave me a big grin. "Yep. I'm officially a college student. In two years, I'll be a registered nurse."

I scooped her up and spun her around in a circle. "Damn, you are gonna look so hot in a nurse's outfit."

She threw back her head and laughed.

"I'm proud of you, sweetheart," I told her when her laughter died away.

"I'm proud of me, too."

"And you're sure you want to keep working at the club? Think you can handle both the class schedule and nights at the Hatter?" I asked. It still amazed me that she even went back there to work. It took her a couple weeks, but then she faced her fears and went back to the club. She said she wouldn't let one bad incident take away all the good memories she had there.

Of course, I had security out the ass now. She was never alone there. Never.

"I'm sure," she said. "If I change my mind, I'll have to put in a call to the boss."

"Hmm," I said, lowering my head. "You can call him anytime."

I captured her lips in a slow and sensual kiss. I kept it light and undemanding, I never wanted her to feel smothered. But this morning, Roxie wanted more. Her fingers dug into my waist and she pressed herself closer, deepening our kiss.

I groaned in the back of my throat as emotions and desire swirled up inside me.

I licked into her mouth, caressing her tongue with mine and nipping at her lower lip. In the back of my head, I willed myself to cool down, but it was so fucking hard.

Her kisses had increasingly become a little more demanding every time. Her touch seemed to burn me a little more, and it was getting harder and harder to pull back.

Roxie slid her hands down my waist and delved her fingertips in the towel at my waist. I stilled and waited for her to pull away.

She didn't. In fact, she gave the soft material a little tug.

I lifted my head and looked at her.

Her fingers continued to tease the edge of the fabric. I put my hand over hers. "Sweetheart, are you trying to drive me crazy?"

"I'm trying to make you want me," she whispered.

My hand jerked over hers. "I always want you. You don't even have to try."

"Even since…?"

"Oh, sweetheart," I drawled. "Nothing could ever make me not want you. You know I'm just giving you the space you need to heal."

"And I love you for it," she said.

I smiled. I never got sick of hearing her say that. It felt like I won the lottery every single time she said those three little words.

"Adam?" she said, stepping a little closer. "I don't want space anymore."

My chest rumbled with the growl that ripped from deep within me. "Are you sure?"

"One hundred percent," she replied.

Anticipation zapped my nerve endings as she led me into the bedroom. The bed was still unmade from this morning, and she stopped at the end.

I lowered to help her tug off her boots, but when she reached for the button on her jeans, I sat on the end of the bed because I wanted her to set the pace.

She slid them off inch by delicious inch, and the towel wrapped around my hips turned into a tent. Her eyes heated when she saw how badly I wanted her, and she quickly pulled off her top and bra.

Her body was perfect. Smooth, creamy skin, curves and full breasts, my hands itched to touch her.

She stepped up in front of me and took my hands, lifting them to her body. I was all too eager to touch her. It seemed as if it had been forever, and I relished the moment and the trust she had in me.

Unable to stop myself, I leaned forward and licked down the center of her abdomen, trailing kisses across her middle. Then I moved over and paid special attention to the tattoo she'd gotten.

"I love this," I murmured, tracing the heart outline with my finger. "I never get tired of seeing this on your body."

Her hand palmed the back of my head and pressed me into it just a little bit harder, and I sucked at her flesh.

The day of the attack, she'd gone to a tattoo parlor before work and had the fading note I'd casually drawn on her made permanent. The word *beach,* had faded away worse than the heart, so she didn't have it put on, but the heart and the *xoxo* were there forever.

She was disappointed she didn't get to surprise me the way she wanted to. Instead, I saw it at the hospital when she was getting treated for her injuries.

But no matter how I first saw it, I loved it. It was a permanent mark between us. The proof that she'd totally become mine.

She told me later that when she'd gotten out of the shower that morning and saw it would disappear soon, she had to do something to save it. She wanted my writing on her forever.

And so it was.

"I love you, Adam," she whispered as I kissed over the heart one more time.

"I love you too, sweetheart," I said as she pushed me back and pulled away the towel.

She climbed over my body and straddled my waist. Her naked torso arching up over me was one of the most beautiful things I would ever see.

"I'm going to drive today," she said as she wrapped her hand around my throbbing cock with a wicked gleam in her eye.

"I'm all yours." I grinned.

"Forever?" she asked.

"Even longer," I vowed.

It was the easiest promise I ever made.

THE END

Ready for more of the *Take It Off* series? Look for **TRACE**, coming fall 2014

I was a girl who vanished without a trace…

I grew up on a tree-lined street, tire swings in every yard and rose bushes lining the white picket fences. As an only child, I was spoiled and the center of my parents' universe. They loved me and I loved them.

Then my dad got sick. He needed a bone marrow transplant to survive. Like any loving daughter, I got tested, knowing deep down I was going to be a match. Knowing I would be the one to save his life.

The day the results came in, I learned I was wrong. I wasn't a match.

But that isn't all I learned.

I also learned he isn't my father.

On his deathbed, he made his confession. He told me who I really was.

I was a girl I'd never met. A girl I didn't know. A girl I now wanted to discover.

I was a girl who was born as someone different and then vanished without a trace.

My name is Keegan Ross, and this is the story of finding me.

**Due to the voices in my head this may or may not be the next release, but rest assured something good is coming soon!*

AUTHOR'S NOTE

This was probably the hardest book in the *Take It Off* series I've had to write to date. My husband would say I say that about *every* book I'm writing at the time, but this one really was the hardest. Up until this point, I would have said *Tempt* was the hardest—if you read my author's note in the back of it, you will know why.

So what made *Trashy* so hard?

Well, first off let me just say (oh boy, I think I'm about to get longwinded… grab onto your hat) that I always said I was going to write a trashy novel. Ha-ha-ha. I think the book itself isn't really a trashy read. It's not one of those books you have to, like, put inside another book when you're out in public so people don't know what you're really reading (at least I hope not!), but I suppose it's my version of a trashy novel, which is basically a guilty pleasure.

I've said this before and I'll say it forever probably, but I write to entertain. I write to give readers a place to escape to from everyday life and reality. That's what I hope you get most out of my books—escapism. Yes, I try to put some underlying emotion in them, but I think all good books need that.

Anyway, even writing to entertain is hard. Some people think writing is easy. I don't agree with that. The only thing easy about my job is that I can do it in my pajamas. That isn't to say I don't love my job, because I do, but some days are really hard.

Trashy is the most requested book in this series. Readers fell in love with Roxie and Adam in *Tease*, which was my second *Take It Off* novel. This book is number ten in the series, so clearly, it took a while for me to get to it, and people have been asking for it for eight books now.

You'd think that would make it easy to write. Wrong. That's one of the reasons it was so challenging. Because Adam and Roxie are so loved, I felt intense pressure to get their story right. I felt intense pressure to deliver Adam the way I know everyone wanted him. He's truly book boyfriend material, isn't he? I had to make him live up to that.

I sort of psyched myself out. I went round and round with the plot on this one, trying to figure out what I wanted to do. I changed my mind several times. I had conflicting thoughts. Usually, I get a plot and run with it. Not so with this one. I worried over this one so much that, as many of you know, I pushed it back a couple times and wrote something else first. Then I got to the point where I was like, *Enough already!* People wanted Adam and I wanted to write him.

It was a struggle to get started. I still wasn't sure where I was going, and I felt like Roxie was somewhat a mystery to me. Her voice was fairly quiet in my loud mind. But I started anyway, and a few chapters in, I decided I needed Adam's point of view. So I started to add him in. And then I realized I didn't know that much about Adam either. I think the biggest question that plagued me about Adam is *why?* Why did he feel the need to get married four times? What makes a guy do that? I didn't want to go the usual his parents had a bad marriage and it affected him. I felt like, for Adam, that was a copout. I didn't want to give him commitment issues, because Adam isn't the type to shy away from hard work or being loyal to the woman he loves. Plus, what man with commitment issues would get married four times? Clearly, he doesn't have commitment issues; he just has problems holding on to his relationships. I was convinced I needed a reason for his marriages, but the more I wrote, the more I wondered if having a reason was really even necessary. Maybe he's just been trying to make that part of his life work, maybe the right girl hadn't come along (until Roxie of course!), and maybe that's all it was. Maybe I was trying to create a big back-story where there wasn't one.

That was hard to accept because part of me is all like, "There needs to be drama!" Maybe Adam is just a drama-free dude. I think we can all appreciate that. Besides, Roxie has enough drama for three people.

I also worried about the plot on this one. I know many of my *Take It Off* novels are action packed, and they start from page one and go, go, go, but like *Tryst,* this one is a little different. Yes, Roxie is struggling against Craig and breaking free of that relationship, but really, *Trashy* isn't about the suspense of what Craig is going to do to her, because he's already been doing crap to her for years. It's more about her internal struggle with it all, how to get away from him, how to accept she can't save everyone. About how to let herself love someone again.

I don't expect everyone to get this book—and trust me; that's hard to say because I want everyone to love Adam and Roxie. But I think when we are dealing with this kind of abuse, not everyone understands the reasons a woman stays. I hope with Roxie, I evoked that kind of understanding of the kind of struggle she went through. She knew it wasn't right, but she just couldn't get out.

Breaking that kind of cycle is hard, especially at that young of an age. And yeah, I'm speaking from experience. More experience than I planned to put into this book, but out it came, and I realized I related to Roxie on a very deep level.

On that note, I really hope people don't criticize her, because I will likely take it personally. On another note, NO, no one ever tried to make me do a porn. LOL! That part is made up. Ha-ha-ha. Drama, people, drama. (Oh, and I've never been a stripper either.)

But the more I wrote, the more poured out of me. Along about thirty thousand words in, I started to become obsessed with this book. I walked around with bloodshot eyes (my kids thought I was sick) because I was so in my head that being in the outside world was too hard. It's a juggling act, trying to live in two different worlds at once. I started worrying less about the plot and just wrote it the way Adam and Roxie told me.

Still, I'm a little nervous to put this baby out into the world. Adam and Roxie… they're my favorite *Take It Off* couple besides Nathan and Honor in *Text*. Adam (to me) is so swoon worthy, and I really, really hope I did him justice for you guys. I hope I gave you everything you wanted in this book, because Lord knows y'all have been asking for it, and I've put a lot of pressure on myself to get it right.

Oh, and by the way, is the cover not absolute perfection?

My kids might disagree with that only because they wanted me to put LSP from *Adventure Time* (it's a TV show) on the cover. LSP stands for Lumpy Space Princess (I'm so serious right now, lol) and she is basically a purple cloud with arms and she talks like a

Valley girl (no offense to all you Valley girls!). LSP likes to say she is going to "write a trashy novel" and it's going to be "like soo trashy." So in my children's minds, LSP would have been the perfect candidate. Ha-ha-ha.

But seriously. This cover is like epic (even without LSP). Thanks to Regina at Mae I Design for creating the beauty.

And thanks to my editor Cassie for making it read good. :-)

I gotta tell you, it feels good to get this book off my list. I really hope you all get where I was going with this story. And I hope you keep reading my books.

I'll see you next book!

XOXO — *Cambria*

Cambria Hebert

Cambria Hebert is a bestselling novelist of more than twenty books. She went to college for a bachelor's degree, couldn't pick a major, and ended up with a degree in cosmetology. So rest assured her characters will always have good hair. She currently resides in North Carolina with her children (human and furry) and her husband, who is a United States Marine.

Besides writing, Cambria loves a caramel latte, staying up late, sleeping in, and watching movies. She considers math human torture and has an irrational fear of chickens (yes, chickens). You can often find her running on the treadmill (she'd rather be eating a donut), painting her toenails (because she bites her fingernails), or walking her chorkie (the real boss of the house).

Cambria has written within the young adult and new adult genres, penning many paranormal and contemporary titles. Her favorite genre to read and write is romantic suspense. A few of her most recognized titles are: *Text, Torch, Tryst, Masquerade,* and *Recalled.*

Cambria Hebert owns and operates Cambria Hebert Books, LLC.

You can find out more about Cambria
and her titles by visiting the links below:

Website: http://www.cambriahebert.com.
Email: cambriahebert@rocketmail.com
Facebook: http://smarturl.co/CambriaHebertFanpage
Twitter: https://twitter.com/cambriahebert
Pinterest: https://pinterest.com/cambriahebert/pins/

www.ingramcontent.com/pod-product-compliance
Lightning Source LLC
Chambersburg PA
CBHW061525210726
48287CB00006B/1833